LIBER EXUVIA

Liber Exuvia

Written & Illustrated by

Elytron Frass

gnOme

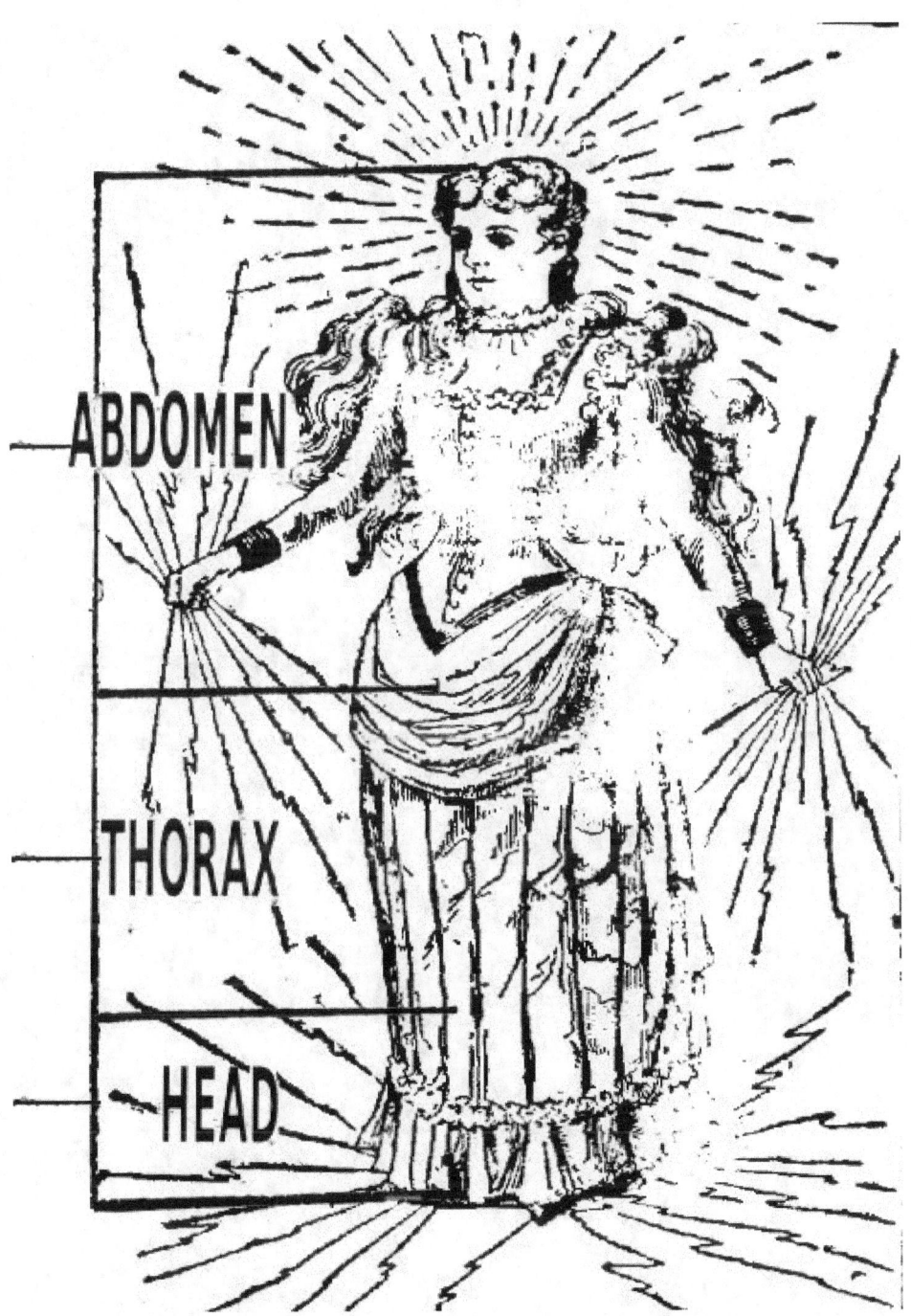

ABDOMEN

Synopsis of Statements
Indicative of a Shared Past Life Regression

Frass, Elytron / You

1. Long ago, I was someone else_____**N/**

2. I was some*thing*_____**Y/**

3. Female_____**Y/**

4. Born from one of one hundred and eight eggs_____**Y/**

5. Cannibalized many of my siblings_____**Y/**

6. Sexually matured beyond my life span's final molt_____**Y/**

7. Had an exoskeleton of iridescent gold_____**Y/**

8. Blended in with my surroundings_____**N/**

9. Was flanked by two pursuers_____**Y/**

10. One: a male of my sp._____**Y/**

11. The other: a giant_____**Y/**

12. It walked upright on two of its four limbs_____**Y/**

13. It gripped a mason jar with noxious poison at its base_____**Y/**

14. They both desired to mount me but in different ways_____**Y/**

15. Respectively, their nostrils/spiracles panted lust hued heat_____**Y/**

16. Their simple/compound eyes ogled my six, slender, chitin-coated legs_____**Y/**

17. Male of my sp. lusted for the swift annihilation of his head for optimal release_____**Y/**

18. Any other day I would have obliged him_____**Y/**

19. Chawing, devouring, and glutting_____**Y/**

20. I would have absorbed him into my eggs_____**Y/**

21. To recycle as cannibal spawn_____**Y/**

22. I could have accepted my alternate fate as a specimen_____**Y/**

23. Could've surrendered myself to the giant_____**Y/**

24. But I was no longer a typical insect_____**Y/**

25. I can explain how, when, where, and why this change within me occurred_____**N/**

26. I somehow ignited with inexplicable crystal clear cognizance_____**Y/**

27. No longer coldblooded nor slow-to-warm_____**Y/**

28. While caught in between my competing pursuers_____**Y/**

29. I realized the paths of ascent and descent_____**Y/**

30. Between an illusory conflict _____**Y/**

31. I stood still as death_____**Y/**

32. A skeletal thing of three segments_____**Y/**

33. Caught between two unequivocal however synchronized lives_____**Y/**

34. I prayed_____**N/**

35. Preyed_____**Y/**

36. Upon them_____**N/**

37. For them_____**N/**

38. For myself_____**N/**

39. On myself_____**Y/**

40. With sharp teeth of my claws I lopped off my own head_____**Y/**

41. Detached from my body and set my blood free_____**Y/**

42. All three of our mouths could drink from its streams_____**Y/**

43. A ménage à trois: space, causality, time_____**Y/**

CIRCLE THE MOST APPLICABLE ANSWER:

I DON'T RECALL ANY OF THIS   =   **-1**

I REMEMBER IT ALL   =   **+1**

Synopsis of Statements

Indicative of a Shared Past Life Regression

Frass, Elytron / You

1. Long ago, I was someone else_____**Y**/

2. My name was Manami Amori_____**Y**/

3. My gender was female, and I was Japanese_____**Y**/

4. I lived with a distant uncle named, Suehiro [Tsukamoto]_____**Y**/

5. I lived with a distant uncle named, [Suehiro] Tsukamoto_____**N**/

6. He was a talented painter of *ukiyo-e*_____**Y**/

7. Made a living off of Katsushika Hokusai forgeries_____**Y**/

8. We resided in post-war [Kyoto] Japan_____**Y**/

9. We resided in post-war Kyoto [Japan]_____**Y**/

10. My parents died in The Great Fire of Bunka_____**Y**/

11. They were incinerated, along with twelve hundred others_____**Y**/

12. I'd often think about them_____**N**/

13. My uncle's home was small and bare_____**Y**/

14. We rarely talked_____**Y**/

15. He was not much older than me_____**N**/

16. I was twenty-two and still a virgin_____**Y**/

17. Despite this, it was easy finding suitors_____**N**/

18. Spent most of my personal time masturbating in my room_____**Y**/

19. Fantasized about great fires spreading out from Edo to Kyoto_____**Y**/

20. I was expected to cook and housekeep for Suehiro_____**Y**/

21. Was content with these duties_____**Y/**

22. I found comfort in repetition and conformity, safety in small spaces_____**Y/**

23. Maintained an array of paper craft hobbies in my spare time_____**N/**

24. I dubbed myself the heir and empress to a peaceful isolation_____**?/**

25. I rarely wished to leave the house_____**Y/**

26. Gave uncle little choice but to carry out the shopping by himself_____**Y/**

27. He'd complain that I should be more sociable_____**Y/**

28. Our neighbors did not like us_____**Y/**

29. I frequently awoke from nightmares in cold sweats_____**Y/**

30. Would often scream unconsciously and wake the neighbors_____**Y/**

31. They'd gossip about *Yōsei* (bewitching spirits) residing in our home_____**?/**

32. Often, we were visited by a specific guest_____**Y/**

33. Guest was Suehiro's friend, Kazako-san_____**Y/**

34. Together they would polish off a pail of sake_____**Y/**

35. Transformed into a pair of rowdy, vulgar drunks_____**Y/**

36. Years prior they attended art school together_____**Y/**

37. Kazako-san was specialized in *Shunga* (erotic subject) painting_____**Y/**

38. Many of his works depicted women having intercourse with insects_____**Y/**

39. He was very generous and kind_____**Y/**

40. For my twenty-second birthday he surprised me with a pet_____**Y/**

41. A pair of mantids in a golden cage_____**Y/**

42. A level of discomforting intensity projected from their compound eyes_____**Y/**

43. Didn't like the way their gazes fixed on me at any given angle_____**Y/**

44. I took them to my room but set them free outside my window_____**Y/**

45. In the parlor, Uncle Suehiro offered me a bowl of sake_____**Y/**

46. I refused_____**N/**

47. I didn't like the taste_____**N/**

48. It made me feel not quite myself_____**Y/**

49. The two of them drank more than usual that night_____**Y/**

50. They'd passed out in the living room_____**Y/**

51. I stumbled drunk and sloth-like to my bedroom_____**Y/**

52. The candlelight was flickering out_____**Y/**

53. In the darkness I was motionless_____**Y/**

54. Felt gradual compression on my chest under an invisible but crushing weight_____**Y/**

55. Lost feeling in my limbs_____**Y/**

56. Retained ability to move_____**N/**

57. I'd tried to shout out through clenched teeth for help_____**Y/**

58. I could not ejaculate a word_____**Y/**

59. As the weird men penetrated my room's paper walls_____**Y/**

60. My heart was pierced by nails of crucifying dread_____**Y/**

61. There were two of them_____**Y/**

62. Utterly inhuman_____**Y/**

63. Standing upright_____**Y/**

64. In the nude_____**N/**

65. Wearing nagajuban kimonos_____**Y/**

66. Mantis Beings_____**Y/**

67. Triangle-headed, slender-limbed, and insect-like_____**Y/**

68. Translucent skin emitted golden light_____**Y/**

69. Stared with a discomforting intensity_____**Y/**

70. Enlarged vacuous compound eyes_____**Y/**

71. Raptorial forelegs yielded vicious spines_____**Y/**

72. Each cradled an ootheca_____**Y/**

73. The size of bonburi lanterns_____**Y/**

74. Dripping fertility's ooze_____**Y/**

75. Their guttural Japanese was non-verbal/telepathic_____**Y/**

76. I had been selected as an incubator for their hybrid child_____**Y/**

77. Succumbed to their remote control, my legs shot up and spread_____**Y/**

78. Frightened like an animal, I urinated in my bed_____**Y/**

79. The following interactions were benign_____**N/**

80. With hands like metal forceps they dilated my vagina_____**Y/**

81. One after the other, they deposited their eggs inside_____**Y/**

82. I heard the pressure-releasing *CRUNCH* of my delicate internal bones_____**Y/**

83. The egg sacks rooted in, then settled_____**Y/**

84. I'd become a surrogate to double reversed births_____**Y/**

85. The Mantis Beings scuttled backward_____**Y/**

86. Receded into walls from whence they came_____**Y/**

87. My vision flickered out like waning candlelight_____**Y/**

88. I phased into a death-like sleep_____**Y/**

89. In the morning I regained control of motor function_____**Y/**

90. Peeled myself from bedsheets—soaked with sweat and urine_____**Y/**

91. Like a classically conditioned housewife, I walked straight into the kitchen_____**Y/**

92. Set the table for Suehiro, Kazako-san, and me_____**Y/**

93. Prepared a congee (rice gruel) breakfast_____**Y/**

94. My porridge cooled and then congealed within its bowl_____**Y/**

95. Waited for an hour before searching every room_____**Y/**

96. The house was empty, quiet_____**Y/**

97. I was home alone_____**Y/**

98. He could have set out early with Kazako-san to sell some paintings_____**Y/**

99. Yet all their depraved artworks were still inside the living room_____**Y/**

100. Wasn't sure what time he would return_____**Y/**

101. The neighbors spoke of saucers hovering above our home_____**?/**

102. I avoided speaking to the neighbors_____**Y/**

103. Waited in the house for thirty-seven weeks_____**Y/**

104. Within this time, my menstrual cycle didn't come_____**Y/**

105. Belly swelled with unborn life_____**Y/**

106. Suehiro [or Kazako-san] eventually returned_____**N/**

107. [Suehiro or] Kazako-san eventually returned_____**N/**

108. Smelled the pus filled stench of my postpartum horrors seeping out_____**Y/**

109. Then died in child labor_____**N/**

110. I gave birth in a warm bath of water without help_____**Y/**

111. To a pair of hybrid twins_____**N/**

112. To Suehiro's and Kazako-san's dismembered heads_____**Y/**

113. I shouted: *hideous abominations!*_____**Y/**

114. Tossed them in the garbage bin_____**Y/**

115. I decided to leave home_____**Y/**

116. After setting fire to Suehiro's house and all of its perverted paintings_____**Y/**

117. Fled the scene_____**Y/**

118. Before my neighbors could suspect me of committing arson_____**Y/**

119. Became a vagabond_____**N/**

120. The authorities caught up with me_____**Y/**

121. It was two days later_____Y/

122. I was somewhere along Tōkaidō road_____Y/

123. This road brought travelers from Edo to Kyoto, and vice versa_____Y/

124. I was caught flirting with a lit bonburi in my hands_____Y/

125. It was Bonburi-matsuri (Bonburi Festival)_____N/

126. My arson spread throughout the neighborhood, I was informed_____Y/

127. The official number of fatalities were undetermined_____Y/

128. Spent the rest of life incarcerated_____Y/

129. Eventually the bodies of Suehiro and Kazako-san were found_____N/

130. I was revisited by Mantis Beings_____N/

CIRCLE THE MOST APPLICABLE ANSWER:

I DON'T RECALL ANY OF THIS   =   -1

I REMEMBER IT ALL   =   +1

Synopsis of Statements

Indicative of a Shared Past Life Regression

Frass, Elytron / You

1. Long ago, I was someone else_____**Y**/

2. My name was Beena Saini_____**Y**/

3. I lived by the central coast of Kathmandu_____**Y**/

4. My father, his father, and his father's father were florists by trade_____**Y**/

5. My father's fingers were riddled with pinpoint wounds from thorns_____**Y**/

6. His hands, stained green by the chlorophyllous blood of stems and leaves____**Y**/

7. Each morning he'd place fresh rhododendrons in my hair_____**Y**/

8. One day I'd become a florist like my father_____**N**/

9. My gender was female, and I was Nepalese_____**Y**/

10. I was bound to house chores like my mother and her mother_____**Y**/

11. And her mother's mother_____**Y**/

12. I was an efficient homemaker_____**N**/

13. Prone to frequent grand mal seizures_____**Y**/

14. Accompanied by visual hallucinations_____**N**/

15. Accompanied by auditory hums_____**N**/

16. Accompanied by olfactory hallucinations_____**Y**/

17. Typically the smell was similar to burning plastic_____**Y**/

18. Parents were protective but attentive, kind, and lenient_____**Y**/

19. I was only allowed to leave our home for funerals and weddings_____**Y**/

20. Attended each of my four older sisters' weddings_____**Y/**

21. Was also present when they laid my little brother on the charnel ground____**Y/**

22. Stayed to watch his body decompose_____**N/**

23. Went into convulsions once or twice a day_____**Y/**

24. Parents worried I'd be difficult to marry off_____**Y/**

25. This was something they'd discuss at night, assuming I was sleeping_____**Y/**

26. Spent my idle moments gazing out the windows_____**Y/**

27. Fantasized about the prospects of a suitor and/or husband_____**N/**

28. Considered running far away from home_____**Y/**

29. From my bedroom window I could see the whole plantation_____**Y/**

30. Beyond our rhododendrons I could see the service road_____**Y/**

31. One evening a traveling stagecoach had pulled over to the shoulder_____**Y/**

32. A gaudy logo, painted on the hood_____**Y/**

33. It read: *The Lowly Dalits' Mobile Freakshow*_____**Y/**

34. Dalits were a people of the lowest caste_____**Y/**

35. They put up a large domed tent with flashy lights_____**Y/**

36. Upon an empty lot across the road_____**Y/**

37. A man atop an elephant was advertising via megaphone_____**N/**

38. I spotted many of the local families lining up to enter_____**Y/**

39. I begged mother and/or father to take me to the midnight show_____**N/**

40. I waited until I was sure that they were sleeping_____**Y/**

41. Snuck out through the first floor window near the backside of our house____**Y/**

42. Avoided each of our four guard dogs, prowling_____**N/**

43. I alarmed them…touching ground with a bombastic *THUD*_____**Y/**

44. Made the swiftest b-line, for the glowing dome tent, that I could_____**Y/**

45. Father jettisoned from bed—preparing to inspect the scene_____ **Y/**

46. The moon provided little light_____**N/**

47. I heard the dogs pursuing—barking wildly behind_____ **Y/**

48. They'd caught up to me beyond the rhododendron fields_____ **N/**

49. Dragged me back home by my throat _____**N/**

50. I continued running for the big top tent and did not dare look back_____ **Y/**

51. I made it safely to the sideshow_____**Y/**

52. Penniless and giddy; surging with adrenaline_____**Y/**

53. The tattoo-faced ticket-checker in the top hat let me in for free_____ **Y/**

54. Smacked his lips and mentioned something about "ladies' night"_____ **?/**

55. A dark brown dwarf escorted me beyond a golden curtain_____**Y/**

56. Colored lights and incense filled the air_____**Y/**

57. I inhaled sandalwood and exhaled frankincense_____**Y/**

58. We passed the Bearded Woman, Human Tumor, and The Lizard Boy_____**Y/**

59. Musicians played the tabla and the flute_____**Y/**

60. I was told to stand among the spectators who waited by a large black stage__**Y/**

61. The spotlight beamed in the shape of a yantra_____**?/**

62. The spotlight focused on a pair of teenage girls_____**Y/**

63. Who had wet and curly unkempt hair_____**Y/**

64. They wore brightly colored patchwork skirts_____**N/**

65. They were unclothed_____**Y/**

66. Only garlands of mammals' skulls partly covered their bare breasts_____**Y/**

67. Each garland made of fifty little skulls_____**?/**

68. One girl was black as coal; one was pale as ash_____**Y/**

69. Both were brandishing a scimitar_____**Y/**

70. I couldn't help but ogle at the sight of their weird beauty_____ **Y/**

71. They received no introduction_____ **N/**

72. A megaphone announced their names: Mekhala and Kanakhala_____ **Y/**

73. They held up their glinting blades for everyone to see_____ **Y/**

74. Their jaws unnaturally unhinged to swallow_____ **Y/**

75. Their scimitars' curvaceous widths were swallowed to the hilts_____ **Y/**

76. Pulled out slowly from blade-engorged throats_____ **Y/**

77. metal screeching between teeth_____ **Y/**

78. I received the wet electric pulses of arousal in my softening pudendum_____ **Y/**

79. As everyone applauded_____ **Y/**

80. Once again, the two girls held their curvy blades up in the air_____ **Y/**

81. Audience gasped, anticipating: '*what on Earth could possibly come next?*'___ **?/**

82. Slack jawed/stunned in silent awe_____ **Y/**

83. Light reflected off the blades_____ **Y/**

84. Struck me harshly in the eyes_____ **Y/**

85. Ushered in [tonic] muscle tension and a neurologic aura_____ **Y/**

86. Quickly followed by fierce [clonic] spasms_____ **Y/**

87. Fear was palpable_____ **Y/**

88. Fear was titillating_____ **Y/**

89. Throat had instantly gone dry_____ **Y/**

90. A bludgeoning headache_____ **Y/**

91. Hyperventilation_____ **Y/**

92. Bilateral paralysis of legs_____ **Y/**

93. A strong smell, which no one seemed to be detecting but myself_____ **Y/**

94. A noxious burning plastic_____ **N/**

95. Maybe rotten eggs_____?/

96. I experienced my body falling, but I never kissed the floor_____Y/

97. Next thing I knew, I was in a different place_____Y/

98. At the edge of a stone stairway_____Y/

99. It led down to the brackish water of the Bagmati River_____Y/

100. Where the dead were bathed—prior to their open-flame cremations_____Y/

101. The grounds were littered with wooden stakes and stained white linens____Y/

102. Linens reminded me of skins shed off in metamorphosis_____?/

103. On an embankment, in the center of the river, corpses burned on pyres____Y/

104. I waded through the river_____Y/

105. Water higher than my knees in depth_____Y/

106. Where loose intestines slithered by like eels_____Y/

107. My bare feet plodding onto the embankment _____Y/

108. From its soil sprung a garden of dismembered limbs_____Y/

109. In the center of the landmass, a decapitated pair of female bodies stood____Y/

110. One was black as pitch—the other, pale as ash_____Y/

111. I recognized them as Mekhala and Kanakhala_____Y/

112. Skull garlands hung around their necks_____N/

113. Their necks were severed off_____Y/

114. Their left hands brandished scimitars_____Y/

115. Their own heads dangled by the unkempt hair within their rights_____Y/

116. Eyes and mouths were closed_____N/

117. An acute awareness and vitality illuminated both their faces_____Y/

118. Tongues protruded out and in like thrusting swords_____Y/

119. Their clean-cut necks began to spurt_____Y/

120. Two thin bloody jets shot up into the air_____**Y/**

121. I recoiled in repulsion_____**N/**

122. From my insides: drooled erogenous secretions_____**Y/**

123. In awe and appetence: I genuflected_____**N/**

124. I sat down between them, at their feet, in lotus_____**Y/**

125. Disembodied toes and fingers mixed in with the ashes on the ground_____**?/**

126. I set my sights skyward_____**Y/**

127. Eyes trained on those twin sanguine streams_____**Y/**

128. Lips parted like a bud, blossoming to bloom_____**Y/**

129. Spreading like a lotus flower_____**N/**

130. Gaping like the rhododendron thirsts before the rain_____**Y/**

131. In all my life I'd never been so thirsty_____**Y/**

132. Their bloodstreams bell-curved downward from on high_____**Y/**

133. Flowed into the flower of my throat_____**Y/**

134. A conduit conjoining two opposing blood types blended into a new third__**Y/**

135. A hybrid sentience swelling in my diaphragm_____**Y/**

136. Both lungs: nourished equally_____**Y/**

137. Awoke upon the floor, underneath the sideshow's dome_____**N/**

138. Among the frantic feet of panicking spectators_____**N/**

139. Awoke in a sickroom_____**Y/**

140. An intensive care unit in West Berlin_____**Y/**

141. It was atypical for me to wake up in a random hospital, post-seizure_____**N/**

142. Figured that my seizures were the reason I was here_____**Y/**

143. I was cocooned in bed sheets_____**Y/**

144. Made to feel secure_____**Y/**

145. The room: white, mostly bare_____**Y/**

146. No clocks or mirrors anywhere_____**Y/**

147. A single painting on the wall_____**Y/**

148. Depicted valkyries, fairies, and elves charging through the skies_____**Y/**

149. Charging to the Earth in hot pursuit of men and beasts_____**Y/**

150. The placard below it read, *Wilde Jagd*_____**Y/**

151. I couldn't place when or where I'd seen this scene before_____**Y/**

152. Waited hours for my father and my mother to arrive_____**Y/**

153. They came eventually_____**N/**

154. A nurse walked in with an investigator_____**Y/**

155. The nurse was a short woman_____**Y/**

156. Was silent_____**Y/**

157. The investigator was a tall man_____**Y/**

158. Dressed in black_____**Y/**

159. He asked if my memories returned_____**Y/**

160. Asked my name, date of birth, and gender_____**Y/**

161. The latter portion of his question was peculiar_____**Y/**

162. But I answered anyway—the answers which I knew as true and honest____**Y/**

163. The nurse and the man in black shook their heads_____**Y/**

164. In affirmation_____**N/**

165. Filled my heart with worry_____**Y/**

166. The investigator asked me to recount whatever I'd last done or seen_____**Y/**

167. I told him everything I could_____**Y/**

168. About the sideshow that had come to town, my seizure, and my visions___**Y/**

169. I was midway into finishing my statement_____**Y/**

170. But the nurse interrupted_____**Y/**

171. Scanned me up and down—a look of pity and disgust_____**Y/**

172. Said: *false memories and gender dysphoria are very common symptoms*___**Y/**

173. *Post-abduction*_____**Y/**

174. I had a chance to process this peculiar line before they left the room_____**N/**

175. I ripped off the bed sheets in a flight of panic_____**Y/**

176. My hands tore off the sheets_____**Y/**

177. My hands were masculine, foreign, and white_____**Y/**

178. I examined my body_____**Y/**

179. My clueless mind was jolted by white knuckle shocks_____**Y/**

180. A foreign prick was jutting out_____**Y/**

181. Between my now-revoltingly Caucasian legs_____**Y/**

CIRCLE THE MOST APPLICABLE ANSWER:

I DON'T RECALL ANY OF THIS   =   **-1**

I REMEMBER IT ALL   =   **+1**

Synopsis of Statements

Indicative of a Shared Past Life Regression

Frass, Elytron / You

1. Long ago, I was someone else_____**Y/**

2. My gender was male, and I was of African descent_____**Y/**

3. I do not recall my birth name _____**Y/**

4. I had no living family_____**?/**

5. Was bought and sold so many times that I couldn't recall my parents' faces_____**Y/**

6. Penultimate master was a Frenchman_____**Y/**

7. Had no living heirs_____**Y/**

8. Died from aneurysm_____**Y/**

9. In an outhouse on the toilet_____**Y/**

10. His land and I were seized by local government_____**Y/**

11. Was mandated to join the Battle of New Orleans_____**Y/**

12. Fought alongside pirates, Injuns, whites, and kindred slaves_____**Y/**

13. Fought proudly for America_____**N/**

14. Survived by lying with the fallen in a swamp_____**Y/**

15. The corpses stunk of Yankee blood_____**N/**

16. The dead were mostly British troops_____**Y/**

17. For ten days I stewed within a casserole of mud and men and bodily fluids_____**Y/**

18. Confronted by the Devil's many forms_____**Y/**

19. Four and six legged_____**Y/**

20. Scavenging vermin_____**Y/**

21. I was quick to learn their ways_____?/

22. Some were crawling on the surface of a book splayed on the battlefield_____Y/

23. Brushed them aside to claim it_____Y/

24. An awful pact was made between us for the sake of my survival_____?/

25. The book was waterlogged but I could still make out its text_____N/

26. Its pages were pristine, yet I couldn't read them_____Y/

27. I wasn't literate_____N/

28. The book was full of foreign glyphs_____Y/

29. I pilfered a gold watch from the pocket of a moldered British bugle boy_____Y/

30. His face, caved in by grapeshot, collected water puddles from the rain_____Y/

31. Opportune mosquitoes had repurposed him: a pond for larval maturation_____Y/

32. The war had ended January 18th, 1815_____Y/

33. Traversed Louisiana on horseback_____N/

34. Became a traveling salesman and daguerreotypist_____N/

35. Before morning, I was inbound towards a free state of the North_____N/

36. Was caught pillaging a dying soldier by a shrewd frontiersman_____Y/

37. Given the choice to hang for petty thievery or to become his cottage slave_____Y/

38. I surrendered to him all my spoils of the war_____Y/

39. The frontiersman took the book, but he couldn't read it either_____Y/

40. Examining the pages, he surmised that it was written in some form of cipher text___Y/

41. He'd give it to his mistress who was good with puzzles and the like_____Y/

42. The cottage stood in the seclusion of a bayou_____Y/

43. Typically he'd leave the doors and windows closed_____N/

44. Invertebrates and rodents always found a way inside_____Y/

45. Knew which insects were considered pests_____N/

46. Knew which ones were considered beneficial_____**N/**

47. My job was to exterminate them all_____**Y/**

48. The frontiersman was a master of knots and bondage rigs_____**Y/**

49. I was always bound to someone or something in the house_____**Y/**

50. He had a flexible and undeveloped mistress_____**Y/**

51. Kept her locked inside a wooden chest_____**Y/**

52. When let out of it, she was a cook, a maid, and a receptacle for sex_____**Y/**

53. She was a pallid Cajun and under legal age to marry_____**Y/**

54. Renamed me, 'The Filet Mignon'_____**N/**

55. We were forbidden to interact outside of sexual relations_____**Y/**

56. The Frontiersman had me lay her as he'd watch_____**Y/**

57. He'd stretch her limbs apart and tie her to the four post bed_____**Y/**

58. I was the tool and proxy for his cruelty_____**Y/**

59. Protested and rebelled_____**N/**

60. I was an obedient and spineless coward_____**Y/**

61. His whip would've cracked a bloody trench into my back_____**Y/**

62. I'd dread the pain in her eyes when she'd let me catch a glimpse of them_____**Y/**

63. Her face and hair would drink up all my body's tears_____**Y/**

64. Self-disgusted with my body as a sweaty rape machine_____**Y/**

65. I'd pray that one day she would grow sharp fangs inside her vaginal canal_____**Y/**

66. Eliminate my pestilential cock in one quick bite_____**Y/**

67. We were products of debasement_____**Y/**

68. In spite of him, we developed ways to signal_____**Y/**

69. A silent language of the damned for comfort and commiseration _____**Y/**

70. Frontiersman's leather lasher: always within right arm's reach_____**Y/**

29

71. Quick to whip me if I'd ease my thrusts or cum too soon_____**Y**/

72. I was an extension of his truncated prurience_____**Y**/

73. He liked to play the cuckhold_____**N**/

74. He was impotent_____**Y**/

75. All that he could do was watch_____**Y**/

76. His mistress cooked three times a day_____**Y**/

77. We'd blink and wink across the room to keep ourselves connected_____**Y**/

78. The three of us would sit together at the table for each meal_____**Y**/

79. Her gumbos were a spiced and savory medley of meats and garden vegetables_____**Y**/

80. Sometimes these ingredients would lead to indigestion_____**Y**/

81. One evening, the frontiersman ran out to the outhouse in flatulent abandon_____**Y**/

82. Momentarily, he left us to our own devices_____**Y**/

83. The Cajun slaved over a boiling stew_____**Y**/

84. She motioned for me as soon as he was gone_____**Y**/

85. Broke silence with an odd request_____**Y**/

86. Asked me to capture bats and rats and puppies, snakes and spiders_____**N**/

87. The discarded skin of a bygone insect stood between the window panes_____**Y**/

88. Asked me to bring it to her quickly_____**Y**/

89. Before our slaver could return_____**Y**/

90. She pulled a book out from the drawer_____**Y**/

91. The book I'd found in battle_____**Y**/

92. Flipping to a certain page—she tapped her finger on an excerpt_____**Y**/

93. She boasted that it took a mere few hours to decode_____**Y**/

94. I couldn't make much sense of it_____**Y**/

95. She read the glyphs with fluency and ease_____**Y**/

96. It was a recipe of sorts_____**Y/**

97. She was willing to divulge its purpose_____**N/**

98. She only hinted that the insect skin was key to an emancipation_____**Y/**

99. An emancipation which would manifest distinctly as our own_____**N/**

100. I pried the window open and procured it_____**Y/**

101. Took a moment to examine this transparent hollow cuticle_____**Y/**

102. I thought: *this could be the opportunity that you'd been waiting for*_____**Y/**

103. We knew which insect it had once belonged to_____**N/**

104. She crushed it into powder via pestle and a mortar_____**Y/**

105. Sprinkled it into the stewing broth_____**Y/**

106. Under nearly silent breath, she whispered_____**Y/**

107. Saying: *Let them find their own way in; let them find their own way out again*____**Y/**

108. Stirred it and prepared three bowls_____**Y/**

109. I had a general knowledge of spells and the occult_____**N/**

110. I imaged that this broth would give us power_____**Y/**

111. Power to break bonds_____**Y/**

112. Power to revolt and flee_____**Y/**

113. Under moonlight, seated by the window, we awaited him_____**Y/**

114. The frontiersman came in panting_____**Y/**

115. Face was sickly green_____**Y/**

116. He struggled to the dinner table set for three_____**Y/**

117. Refused to eat his portion of the stew_____**Y/**

118. His mistress and I finished every spoonful in our bowls_____**Y/**

119. Knew whether the dark spell's onset would be chronic or acute_____**N/**

120. Nausea was a bug: dragging spines along the walls of my intestines_____**Y/**

121. The Cajun cackled, quaked, and sweated_____**Y/**

122. Our bellies were distending_____**Y/**

123. We'd been overcome by uncontrollable hysterics and dry heaves_____**Y/**

124. Labored by a bubbling bloat_____**Y/**

125. The frontiersman jumped out from his seat—unsure of what to do_____**Y/**

126. Alerted by our swollen and continuous expansion_____**Y/**

127. This impregnation which negated reason_____ **Y/**

128. Discomfort was diminishing_____**N/**

129. Inflammation morphed our private parts as well_____**Y/**

130. An exaggerated swelling I'd exhibited before _____**N/**

131. Felt such small but forceful movements stirring from within_____**Y/**

132. These things began to claw inside my abdomen and scrotum_____**Y/**

133. The frontiersman was recoiling—confounded and repulsed_____**Y/**

134. His mistress and I ruptured like the skins of pierced balloons_____**Y/**

135. An ootheca eclipsed the moon_____**Y/**

136. Mantids spilled from each of us_____**Y/**

137. Endlessly, the nymph hordes jettisoned_____**Y/**

138. They filled up every square inch of the room_____**Y/**

139. The three of us were drowned in exoskeletons_____**Y/**

140. This emergence was our nearest parallel to freedom_____**Y/**

CIRCLE THE MOST APPLICABLE ANSWER:

I DON'T RECALL ANY OF THIS   =   **-1**

I REMEMBER IT ALL   =   **+1**

Synopsis of Statements

Indicative of a Shared Past Life Regression

Frass, Elytron / You

1. Long ago, I bifurcated into simultaneous lives_____**Y**/

2. A set of twins_____**Y**/

3. Born in Sedona, Arizona, 1963_____**Y**/

4. In a single family home_____**N**/

5. Raised within a trailer park_____**Y**/

6. We were brothers_____**Y**/

7. Identical_____**N**/

8. Our names were Walter and Wallace_____**Y**/

9. Mother's maiden name was Ward_____**Y**/

10. She was legally divorced_____**N**/

11. Never married_____**Y**/

12. She was typically at work_____**N**/

13. Mostly stayed at home with us_____**Y**/

14. She'd only leave us home alone on weekends_____**Y**/

15. She'd spend her nights two trailers down from ours_____**Y**/

16. With her boyfriends, Steven and César_____**Y**/

17. Her income came from child support_____**N**/

18. Received a monthly Welfare check and food stamps from the government_____**Y**/

19. We were told to sell a portion of the food stamps_____**Y**/

20. For a sum of cash to pay the rent_____**Y**/

21. Mother and her boyfriends drank a lot of beer_____**N/**

22. Preferred experimenting with hallucinogens_____**Y/**

23. Under the fog of a patchouli scented brand of incense_____**Y/**

24. In the presence of quartz crystals_____**Y/**

25. Steven and César drove everywhere together in their car_____**Y/**

26. A 1976 Thunderbird_____**N/**

27. The vehicle was baby blue_____**N/**

28. One Saturday morning they surprised us with a pizza_____**Y/**

29. Sprinkled psilocybin mushrooms on it_____**Y/**

30. Our bodies melded with the furniture_____**Y/**

31. Cartoons were being born out of the television's cyclops eye_____**Y/**

32. Broadcasts ran amok within our living room_____**Y/**

33. We registered the news break warning that a female prisoner escaped from jail_____**N/**

34. Steven, César, and our mother watched us speak in tongues for their amusement____**Y/**

35. Only when our drugs wore off did they begin to do their own_____**Y/**

36. They smoked a pipe with something crystalline inside_____**Y/**

37. Their bodies sprawled then stiffened on the couch_____**Y/**

38. Consciousness receded far behind their undead eyes_____**Y/**

39. Minutes later, they regurgitated newfound presence and awareness_____**Y/**

40. The three of them awoke—quieted and changed_____**Y/**

41. Like sages coming down from mountains after years of isolation_____**Y/**

42. Steven claimed he'd been transported to a mystical domain of fractal light_____**Y/**

43. César was met with bioluminescent swarms of elves_____**Y/**

44. Mother's trip was spammed by psychic advertisements via her pineal gland_____**Y/**

45. Received coordinates to the Akashic Records_____**Y/**

46. A directory of endless knowledge—seated in the interstice of time_____ **Y/**

47. Its access point—a crossroads—known only to the elves_____ **Y/**

48. When the drug lost its effect on us we parted ways_____ **Y/**

49. Mother told us to behave ourselves_____ **Y/**

50. She drove off with her men_____ **Y/**

51. In mom's absence we were always left with yearning and the void_____ **Y/**

52. Her precious drugs were hidden well_____ **N/**

53. We found her stash within the kitchen cupboard_____ **Y/**

54. Among the canned goods in an emptied can of soup_____ **Y/**

55. Labeled 'Cream of Broccoli'_____ **?/**

56. We knew what type of drug it was_____ **N/**

57. We rolled it into a fat cigarette with rolling paper_____ **Y/**

58. We smoked most of it_____ **Y/**

59. Euphoria and poisons burned within our chests_____ **Y/**

60. Our lungs were young and virile_____ **Y/**

61. We had nothing else to do_____ **Y/**

62. Sedona was an International Dark Sky City_____ **Y/**

63. There was virtually no light pollution after sunset_____ **Y/**

64. We dressed in black and cloaked ourselves in darkness_____ **Y/**

65. Laid belly-up outside, nearby the outskirts of the trailer park_____ **Y/**

66. Our eyes adjusted to the powerful illumination of the moon and stars_____ **Y/**

67. The nearby bushes rustled_____ **Y/**

68. Approx. six minutes from the time we finished tripping_____ **Y/**

69. We anticipated the arrival of the elves_____ **Y/**

70. A thing was flung in our direction_____ **Y/**

71. It landed with a muffled thud_____**Y/**

72. It could have been a pebble or a twig_____**N/**

73. That was all it took to shake us from our stupors_____**Y/**

74. We synchronically recoiled as we scanned the dark_____**Y/**

75. We strained our eyes_____**Y/**

76. A bright reflective heap of orange colored clothes lay in the grass before us_____**Y/**

77. We could see—aided only by the stars—the orange uniform was tattered_____**Y/**

78. An interrupting laughter brought our eyes away from it_____**Y/**

79. A gentle cackle—feminine in nature_____**Y/**

80. Its source was cast in shadow_____**Y/**

81. It came out from the nearby shrubs_____**Y/**

82. A vicious long clawed elf_____**N/**

83. A tall and longhaired woman_____**Y/**

84. She was about six feet tall_____**N/**

85. She was about eight feet tall_____**Y/**

86. Her pendulant breasts and buttocks were silhouetted by the moon_____**Y/**

87. She held her hands up high as if she were surrendering_____**Y/**

88. Dropped them once she saw that we were not a threat_____**Y/**

89. Her skin was so much paler than our mom's_____**Y/**

90. Her firm legs towered over us—an inverted gaping 'V'_____**Y/**

91. She put a finger to her lips to keep us hushed_____**Y/**

92. Her hand slid down from them—slowly moving towards her sex_____**Y/**

93. As she began to play with it, we stared like hungry wolves_____**Y/**

94. She squatted down beside us for the climax_____**Y/**

95. Released a violent stream of cum_____**Y/**

96. Followed by a stream of urine_____ **Y/**

97. Chased by a half-coagulated stream of uterine blood_____ **Y/**

98. Bellowed a deep sigh of relief when she was done_____ **Y/**

99. Nodding as a sign of satisfaction without uttering a word_____ **Y/**

100. Blood rushed to the bulges in our pants as it departed from our brains_____ **Y/**

101. The woman stood up from her puddle_____ **Y/**

102. Took us warmly by our hands_____ **Y/**

103. We followed_____ **Y/**

104. Through the backyard wilderness of Arizona_____ **Y/**

105. She used body language to direct us_____ **Y/**

106. Either she was mute or non-English-speaking_____ **?/**

107. We avoided being seen_____ **Y/**

108. The three of us walked, nonstop, until we hit the city's edge_____ **Y/**

109. Where the Verde Canyon Railroad crossed its lines_____ **Y/**

110. We weren't far away from home_____ **N/**

111. Beyond the crossing, one track climbed an overpass back into town_____ **Y/**

112. The other one led to the canyon down below_____ **Y/**

113. We were able to survey our immediate surroundings_____ **N/**

114. It was way too dark to see_____ **Y/**

115. We were standing at a point where many tracks converged_____ **?/**

116. Our naked woman's knees crunched gravel_____ **Y/**

117. She came between us, kneeling down_____ **Y/**

118. Unzipped our trousers_____ **Y/**

119. Calloused hands slid in_____ **Y/**

120. Began to palpate on our balls_____ **Y/**

121. We each grabbed for the silhouetted pleasures of her breasts_____**Y/**

122. But she was quick to back away_____**Y/**

123. Touch, it seemed, was not a mutual exchange_____**Y/**

124. She instructed us to lay down on the ground_____**Y/**

125. She roughly pulled our trousers to our ankles_____**Y/**

126. We ignored the jaggedness of gravel poking at our glutes and backs_____**Y/**

127. Our heads rested on the railroad tracks_____**Y/**

128. With ambidextrous skill, she began to milk our cocks_____**Y/**

129. Our eyes rolled back into a sightless bliss_____**Y/**

130. We surrendered to the rhythm of her tugs_____**Y/**

131. Conjoined as one synchronic system_____**Y/**

132. Ejaculated cum of shimmering and tranquil light_____**Y/**

133. Followed by a gentle flowing piss_____**Y/**

134. Ending with a spritz of blood_____**Y/**

135. She rendered us insensible_____**Y/**

136. Deaf and blind to the approaching train_____**Y/**

137. Its muted wheels passed through us_____**Y/**

138. Infinitudes of fractals scintillated from its light_____**Y/**

139. Our heads were mutually obliterated_____**Y/**

140. The tall woman remained focused on our genitals_____**Y/**

141. Guiding us through incomparable and rapturous heights of orgasm_____**Y/**

142. We retained awareness well into our deaths_____**Y/**

143. With her grip around our joysticks—we were piloted to realms beyond concern___**Y/**

144. Our cadavers fell through vortices of alternating color schemes_____**Y/**

145. And bottomless agendas_____**Y/**

146. We were given total access to the Akashic Records_____**N/**

147. Yet our memories imprinted new and wet-electric pages_____**Y/**

148. Into the vastness and abruptness of its cosmic-mechanical mind_____**Y/**

CIRCLE THE MOST APPLICABLE ANSWER:

I DON'T RECALL ANY OF THIS   =   **-1**

I REMEMBER IT ALL   =   **+1**

Synopsis of Statements

Indicative of a Shared Past Life Regression

Frass, Elytron / You

1. Long ago, I was the infertile wives of a polygamist_____ **Y/**

2. His name was Ngombu [Tejjeh]_____ **Y/**

3. His name was [Ngombu] Tejjeh_____ **N/**

4. Our names were Aicha and Bogdona [Tejjeh]_____ **Y/**

5. Lived under one roof in Monrovia [Liberia]_____ **Y/**

6. In year 1846_____ **?/**

7. During a time when the United States refused to claim sovereignty over us_____ **Y/**

8. Demanded that Liberia declare its independence_____ **Y/**

9. While Whites shipped over droves of ex-slaves to be free_____ **Y/**

10. Many knew who they were, where they came from, and how to assimilate_____ **N/**

11. Embraced by our tribes_____ **N/**

12. They were demoralized_____ **Y/**

13. Husband advocated to segregate Americo-Liberians from our native population____ **Y/**

14. He was ethnically Nedme_____ **Y/**

15. A member of the secret Annelid Society, formed exclusively for men_____ **?/**

16. Funneled his libidinous frustrations through a political hard line_____ **Y/**

17. He suffered from impotence_____ **N/**

18. Dissatisfied with our sexual frigidness and barren wombs_____ **Y/**

19. As much as we were_____ **Y/**

20. As wives, we wished to please him more than anything_____ **Y/**

21. To pleasure him beyond his fantasies_____Y/

22. To bear his sons and daughters_____Y/

23. He'd try to get us in the mood_____Y/

24. With his two fingers_____Y/

25. And/or his tongue_____Y/

26. Such stimuli as this brought nondescript but ugly feelings down below_____Y/

27. During instances of intercourse we'd experience traumatic visions_____Y/

28. Hallucinated insects on our vulvas—feeding _____Y/

29. The endemic *Mantis chinnamundayai,* most likely_____?/

30. When the time would come to lay with him each night we'd feign nausea or fever__Y/

31. Our husband had suspected we were cursed_____Y/

32. This was something modern medicine could fix_____N/

33. He took us far outside the city limits of Monrovia_____Y/

34. To a psychiatric therapist_____N/

35. To the rural forests where the witchdoctors resided in their isolated huts_____Y/

36. We were led into an office_____N/

37. We were led into a hut_____Y/

38. Made of corrugated metal_____N/

39. At the time we'd known that we had been here once before_____N/

40. Greeted by a Majo_____Y/

41. Female leader of the secret Arthropod Society, exclusively for Nedme women_____Y/

42. Her wooden mask concealed her face and head_____Y/

43. Resembled a ferocious mammal_____N/

44. Resembled *Mantis chhinnamastayai*_____?/

45. From her neck down she was cloaked in dry and slender leaves of palm_____Y/

46. The palm was green, not yellow_____**N/**

47. It was *Raphia palma-pinus*_____**?/**

48. She inspected our skin, the inside of our mouths, our eyes_____**Y/**

49. Ascertained our troubles rooted in a curse_____**N/**

50. Certain our condition could be cured_____**N/**

51. She told our husband to go home and get some rest_____**Y/**

52. Our husband was instructed to return within a week to pick us up_____**Y/**

53. We were administered a bubbling decoction_____**Y/**

54. Derived from red palm root_____**?/**

55. Belonging to *E. guineesis*_____**?/**

56. The Majo stood upright—opposite us_____**Y/**

57. Instructed us to sit_____**Y/**

58. Sung a sad familiar song_____**Y/**

59. In the secret language of the Arthropod Society, known only to initiated women____**Y/**

60. We laid upon the hard dirt floor_____**Y/**

61. We held each other's hands_____**Y/**

62. The Majo lifted off her headdress_____**Y/**

63. We recognized the face of an old hag_____**Y/**

64. Her decoction ushered in a death-like sleep_____**Y/**

65. Woke up within a repressed memory of our past_____**Y/**

66. Inside that very room_____**Y/**

67. It was twelve years prior_____**Y/**

68. We were girls who'd just hit puberty_____**Y/**

69. Lying on the hard dirt floor_____**Y/**

70. Our bodies: covered in white clay and hojo [animal fat]_____**Y/**

71. We were drunk on palm wine_____**Y/**

72. Arms and legs spread-eagle_____**Y/**

73. Immobilized by invisible forces_____**Y/**

74. The Majo entered_____**Y/**

75. Wore an insectile headdress_____**Y/**

76. She was naked from neck down_____**N/**

77. Covered from neck down in a gown of black palm leaves_____**Y/**

78. Between her hands she held a blade for carving flesh_____**Y/**

79. Her hands around the blade were clasped in prayer_____**Y/**

80. She chanted in the cryptic language of the Arthropod Society_____**Y/**

81. This was the day of our initiation_____**Y/**

82. It would prep us for adulthood, marriage, and prolific childbearing_____**Y/**

83. We were to be circumcised_____**Y/**

84. The woman's blade was crude but sanctified for surgery_____**Y/**

85. Excised us of clitorises and labia_____**Y/**

86. Our flowing acrid tears canalled into our cheeks_____**Y/**

87. We clenched and ground our teeth so forcefully_____**Y/**

88. They cracked and crumbled into powder in our mouths_____**Y/**

89. Eyes rolled back into our skulls_____**Y/**

90. Remembrance of that white hot pain returned us to the present time_____**Y/**

91. Back inside the doctor-witch's hut_____**Y/**

92. Our frigidness was cured_____**Y/**

93. But reawakened primal appetites not satiated easily_____**Y/**

94. Our pelvises engaged in tribadism _____**Y/**

95. Pelvic bones concealed behind the raw red curtains made from scarred meatuses___**Y/**

96. Our legs were scissoring the Majo's body_____Y/

97. Her dress and headdress were cast off into a pile_____Y/

98. The friction in our frenzied tribbing sloughed off much of her dark skin_____Y/

99. Her bones shattered underneath our lust_____Y/

100. She was smothered, crushed between us_____Y/

101. The hag was breaking, stiffening, and going cold_____Y/

102. We gobbled up her meat before its stink could draw in flies_____Y/

103. We mounted her remains_____Y/

104. Rode her skeleton throughout our stay_____Y/

105. It was a means to bide our restless time_____Y/

106. Awaiting our husband's return_____Y/

107. We hoped that he'd be pleased with our accelerated progress_____Y/

108. We were ready for him either way_____Y/

CIRCLE THE MOST APPLICABLE ANSWER:

I DON'T RECALL ANY OF THIS   =   **-1**

I REMEMBER IT ALL   =   **+1**

Synopsis of Statements

Indicative of Past Life Regression

Frass, Elytron / You

1. Long ago, I was a mutable lover_____**Y/**

2. The instigator of a taboo love triangle_____**Y/**

3. A ménage à trois_____**N/**

4. Each partner thought they had me to themselves_____**Y/**

5. A married couple_____**Y/**

6. Who lived within Masuleh in Gilan [Province in Iran]_____**Y/**

7. Where only binaries were considered ḥalāl_____**Y/**

8. It was 1980_____**Y/**

9. Iran was an outcast in the eye of the world_____**Y/**

10. Gender reassignment was permissible_____**Y/**

11. Remaining intersex was not_____**Y/**

12. The couple that I visited worked and slept on opposite shifts_____**Y/**

13. Their lives seldom overlapped_____**Y/**

14. They became estranged_____**Y/**

15. Considered a divorce_____**N/**

16. An official separation would mar their social statuses for life_____**Y/**

17. Sought my matchless pleasures within peak hours of each other's' absences_____**Y/**

18. Our conjugal visits took place at noon and midnight_____**Y/**

19. Husband worked daytime hours_____**Y/**

20. A book peddler at the village's bazaar_____**Y/**

21. He'd signal for me by leaving his bedroom light on_____**Y/**

22. Wife worked nightshift_____**Y/**

23. A hospital orderly in Shaft, Gilan_____**Y/**

24. She'd make sure to draw the curtains down to let me know she was alone_____**Y/**

25. I was born of a certain phenotype to please everyone and no one_____**Y/**

26. I decided to keep myself a mystery for my protection_____**Y/**

27. Always kept my clothes on during sexual encounters_____**Y/**

28. I'd never receive; I'd only give_____**Y/**

29. I did not wish to be reciprocated_____**N/**

30. Risk outweighed reward_____**Y/**

31. For him, I'd mimic the appearance of his wife_____**N/**

32. For her, I'd mimic the appearance of her husband_____**N/**

33. I'd fuck the husband and the wife as their respective doppelgängers_____**Y/**

34. They desired fornication with a simulacrum of themselves_____**Y/**

35. Mimicked the husband as his domineering double_____**Y/**

36. He'd have me drive my cock so far into his esophagus_____**Y/**

37. I'd unload myself directly in his gut_____**Y/**

38. He would rest his head upon my lap, often vomiting or gagging_____**Y/**

39. I mimicked the wife as her demonic "other half"_____**Y/**

40. She'd welcome my fists into her cunt and rectum_____**Y/**

41. I'd pull out her prolapsed and puckering roses_____**Y/**

42. Kissed and tongued the glistening saline dew from their buds_____**Y/**

43. On the beach I waited_____**Y/**

44. Shed my disguises as if clothes were cast-off skins_____**Y/**

45. From here each home and business could be seen_____**Y/**

46. Masuleh rose like an ischial spine from the bladdery shore of the Caspian Sea_____**Y/**

47. Built up on an incline, into the mountain slope_____**Y/**

48. Its bone yellow buildings and bone yellow homes interconnected_____**Y/**

49. It's said: *"The yards of the buildings above are the roofs of the buildings below"*____**Y/**

50. It had been weeks since our discomforting three-way attempt_____**Y/**

51. Which went nowhere and ended in tears_____**Y/**

52. It was midday_____**Y/**

53. I waited for the wife to show her signal_____**Y/**

54. I was in full garb: gold abaya and hijab—mimicking *her*_____**Y/**

55. My face was painted with makeup_____**Y/**

56. My armpits doused in rosewater spray_____**Y/**

57. Her signal never came_____**Y/**

58. I shed clothing_____**Y/**

59. Washed my feminine scent off with some water from the sea_____**Y/**

60. The night arrived_____**Y/**

61. Waited by the water's edge, staring at a window for the husband's sign to come____**Y/**

62. My hair combed over like his_____**Y/**

63. Dressed in a duplicate of the suit that he'd wear on most days_____**Y/**

64. Mimicking *him*, I observed Masuleh at midnight_____**Y/**

65. On the roof-streets pot and carpet makers packed away their wares_____**Y/**

66. A vagabond musician hammered on his stringed santūr_____**Y/**

67. I saw black lurking dogs: emissaries of the djinn_____**Y/**

68. They rummaged roofs for midnight spoils_____**Y/**

69. Drunken scuffles carried on_____**Y/**

70. From stairways which conjoined the top and bottom housing tiers_____ **Y/**

71. Lit windows to the bars and restaurants packed in with dead-end life_____ **Y/**

72. There were no alleyways_____ **Y/**

73. The only privacy remained within the homes_____ **Y/**

74. Houses stacked upon houses—the streets were their roofs_____ **Y/**

75. I could view all goings-on within the open air bazaar_____ **Y/**

76. Hustlers had nowhere to prowl_____ **Y/**

77. All was exposed_____ **Y/**

78. I hid behind the jutting rocks upon the beach_____ **Y/**

79. Eventually the light turned on_____ **N/**

80. His signal didn't sign_____ **Y/**

81. Morning arrived_____ **Y/**

82. I mimicked the wife again_____ **Y/**

83. Walked to the bookstand within the bazaar_____ **Y/**

84. He was right where he'd always be, peddling his books_____ **N/**

85. Instead, his wife was there working the stall_____ **Y/**

86. We wore the same attire, the same rosewater scent_____ **Y/**

87. Our eyes were lined with an identical cosmetic kohl_____ **Y/**

88. I buried my face in a book before she could register me_____ **Y/**

89. An anthology of essays on *Die Wilde Jagd*_____ **Y/**

90. Translated to Farsi from its original German_____ **Y/**

91. I found a literal refuge between its dense pages_____ **Y/**

92. Its internal spine's creases were pinching my nose_____ **Y/**

93. I regretted not staying back at the beach_____ **Y/**

94. Regretted not being more careful_____ **Y/**

95. The pages were torn from my face_____**Y/**

96. My veil and my wig were plucked off from behind_____**Y/**

97. The husband and wife had ambushed me from opposite sides_____**Y/**

98. A curious market crowd circled around_____**Y/**

99. I was kicked to the ground_____**Y/**

100. When they tore my abaya, I felt searing pain as if it were skin being flayed_____**Y/**

101. Underneath, I was dressed like the husband_____**Y/**

102. They ripped his clothes off of me, and, then, I was fully exposed_____**Y/**

103. My soft humming flesh: forced out from metamorphic integuments_____**Y/**

104. Sundered from the arts of my glamour_____**Y/**

105. Scrutinized by all eyes under stark beaming sunlight_____**Y/**

106. Drooping and blooming: my dual genitalia was_____**Y/**

107. That of a woman and that of a man_____**Y/**

108. Pummeled by fists in the ribs and the groin_____**Y/**

109. Someone handed out cups to the husband and wife_____**Y/**

110. Brimming with vitriolic fluid and fumes_____**Y/**

111. Tossed at my face_____**Y/**

112. Shrieked as the acid chewed into my eyes_____**Y/**

113. I gurgled and foamed_____**Y/**

114. Face melted off like running mascara_____**Y/**

115. My scalp and my actual hair peeled off and plopped onto the floor_____**Y/**

116. My likeness eroded—my skull, denuding_____**Y/**

117. Diluted into a sludge of biochemical waste_____**Y/**

118. The pulp of my head and softening skull liquefied_____**Y/**

119. I melted like plastic caved into my throat_____**Y/**

120. My eyes rolled with loose teeth down its lumen _____Y/

121. Saw the husband and wife staring into my hole_____Y/

122. Fixated; drawn inward_____Y/

123. Asphyxiating stenches seethed out of the void where my head used to be_____Y/

124. Fetid vapors wormed into their nostrils_____Y/

125. Permeated their lungs and mucosa_____Y/

126. I became too repugnant and toxic to bear_____Y/

127. The husband and wife passed out cold at my sides_____Y/

CIRCLE THE MOST APPLICABLE ANSWER:

I DON'T RECALL ANY OF THIS   =   **-1**

I REMEMBER IT ALL   =   **+1**

Synopsis of Statements

Indicative of a Shared Past Life Regression

Frass, Elytron / You

1. Long ago, I was an ontological failure_____**Y/**

2. Lived within the forest at the edge of town_____**Y/**

3. In Tanacu_____**N/**

4. In Transylvania_____**N/**

5. Somewhere in Romania_____**Y/**

6. My name was Radu [Cantemir]_____**N/**

7. My name was [Radu] Cantemir_____**N/**

8. Born January, 2, 1973_____**?/**

9. I was once a youthful but authoritative steward of the Lord_____**Y/**

10. A residing monk who led a female monastery_____**Y/**

11. Later on defrocked and excommunicated_____**Y/**

12. After serving seven years in prison, I was exiled to the forest_____**Y/**

13. In desolation, prayed for an exact comeuppance_____**Y/**

14. One summer's night, in 1995, my prayers were finally answered_____**Y/**

15. By the Lord whom all my prayers went out to_____**N/**

16. There was a fence around my humble cottage_____**Y/**

17. Where I self-sustained on vegetables I'd grown and chickens that I'd raised_____**Y/**

18. Fiery meteors were raining overhead_____**Y/**

19. I observed them from my window_____**Y/**

20. They pocked and carbonized the earth around them_____**Y/**

21. Where they landed with a thunderous crash_____**Y/**

22. My chickens clucked and flapped their wings as if this meant their doom_____**Y/**

23. The cottage roof was spared_____**Y/**

24. I waited until morning to have a look outside_____**Y/**

25. The chickens had been barbecued along with all my crops_____**Y/**

26. In the center of the garden stood a hulking rock from space_____**Y/**

27. I was awestruck_____**Y/**

28. Less saddened by my livestock's fate_____**Y/**

29. More surprised that my abode did not go up in flames_____**Y/**

30. With cautious reverence I approached the hulking rock_____**Y/**

31. Upon closer inspection I could see that it was just an ordinary lump of matter_____**N/**

32. It was covered in strange glyphs etched into the surface_____**Y/**

33. I recalled the many grimoires shown to me in seminary school_____**Y/**

34. *The Key of Hell* by Cyprianus_____**Y/**

35. John Dee's *Liber Logaeth*_____**Y/**

36. *The Sixth and Seventh Book of Moses*_____**Y/**

37. An entire class was dedicated to the semiotics and translations of these books_____**Y/**

38. I spent the following weeks deciphering my stone_____**Y/**

39. There were less constructive ways to spend my time_____**Y/**

40. I managed to identify its code of twenty-seven glyphs_____**Y/**

41. Four letters shy of our Romanian alphabet_____**Y/**

42. Too numerous to coincide with Hebrew_____**Y/**

43. English was a likely candidate, although a letter shy_____**Y/**

44. Then I remembered Johannes Trithemius' Theban Alphabet (written, 1518)_____**Y/**

45. Used its final alphabetic symbol as a stand-in for a period to end each sentence_____**Y/**

46. I applied this to the twenty-seventh glyph_____**Y/**

47. Furthermore, it functioned as a placeholder between each word_____**Y/**

48. I then aligned the rest of them, from one through twenty-six, with English letters___**Y/**

49. To self-congratulate, I chose to read the stone-etched words aloud_____**Y/**

50. *Danse, Dragaice, Valve, Iezme, Izme, Irodite, Rusalii, Nagode, Vântoase, Domnite,*

    Maiestre, Frumoase, Musate, Fetele Codrului, Imparatesele Vazduhului, Zanioare,

    Sfinte de Noapte, Soimane, Mandre, Fecioare, Albe, and *Hale*_____**Y/**

51. I recognized these names which were not names but epithets and incantations_____**Y/**

52. Of a collective female spirit known as *They,* or *Iele* in Romanian_____**Y/**

53. Which moved in groups of three or seven_____**Y/**

54. And appeared to lost or wandering men as virginal seductresses_____**Y/**

55. As soon as their epithets left my lips the rock began to quake_____**Y/**

56. It was being cracked and burst out from within_____**Y/**

57. I was free of fear, and I continued edging closer as it hatched_____**Y/**

58. It would not have mattered if it birthed a horde of devils nor a host of angels_____**Y/**

59. After all, I figured, I had nothing left to gain or lose_____**Y/**

60. As the creatures were emerging I made sure to be the first thing they laid eyes on___**Y/**

61. Emerging from the egg-like stone, the two appeared_____**Y/**

62. More alien than anything that my wildest dreams could imagine_____**Y/**

63. Profane collages of human and insect proportions_____**Y/**

64. One, standing tall as myself, had the virile body of a girl_____**Y/**

65. But the green head of a mantis_____**Y/**

66. The other was no larger than a housecat as it balanced on six legs_____**Y/**

67. With the face of a young woman and the body of a mantis_____**Y/**

68. Its serrated forelegs folded over and held up high as if engaged in prayer_____ **Y/**

69. Their piercing yet unsympathetic eyes locked onto me_____ **Y/**

70. I made sure to gaze just as intensely back at them_____ **Y/**

71. Spreading mouthparts wide, they rasped the hymn of beings fallen from the stars___ **Y/**

72. They sang, *ALL WHO CONJURE IELE FALL INTO CERTAIN RUIN AND DESPAIR*___ **Y/**

73. I informed these creatures that I had already come to peace with this idea_____ **Y/**

74. But requested just one favor in return_____ **Y/**

75. That Iele send me back in time_____ **Y/**

76. In order to prevent my younger self from making an unpardonable error_____ **Y/**

77. That dehumanizing act which led to his/my banishment_____ **Y/**

78. I'd be willing to murder him/myself were it the only resolution_____ **Y/**

79. I wasn't sure they understood_____ **Y/**

80. However, without warning, Iele started to emit a putrid light_____ **Y/**

81. My skin burned in the presence of their bioluminescence_____ **Y/**

82. Which strobed until it blinded me_____ **Y/**

83. My eyes reopened in another place and time_____ **Y/**

84. Iele fulfilled my wishes_____ **Y/**

85. But not as I expected_____ **Y/**

86. They towered over me_____ **Y/**

87. One of Iele swapped her insect head for that of a familiar man's_____ **Y/**

88. The other swapped her insect body for his own_____ **Y/**

89. They wore those sections of my body like an unhemmed suit_____ **Y/**

90. I stood in the grass at their feet looking up_____ **Y/**

91. Transformed into a were-mantis—diminutive in size_____ **Y/**

92. I retained my mental faculties, at least_____ **Y/**

93. And negotiated for the ability of human speech_____**Y/**

94. I would have rather given them my soul_____**Y/**

95. But they saw little value in that kind of exchange_____**Y/**

96. They were only interested in my flesh_____**Y/**

97. They'd return me to my normal state upon achievement of my goals_____**Y/**

98. Iele pointed to the monastery in the foreground_____**Y/**

99. Before evaporating on thin air_____**Y/**

100. It was sometime in late spring or early summer_____**Y/**

101. I waited, still as death, for dawn_____**Y/**

102. My self of ten years younger left his bedroom window open at this time_____**Y/**

103. From that point of entry, I crept into his room_____**Y/**

104. Mother Superior arrived each morning to awake him_____**Y/**

105. He'd officiate the morning mass_____**Y/**

106. He had not been woken up yet_____**Y/**

107. He was snoring in his sleep_____**Y/**

108. I clambered up his bed_____**Y/**

109. Crawled along his body_____**Y/**

110. Darkly casting a nightmarish shadow on his far right wall_____**Y/**

111. I crept up delicately past his bright red beard_____**Y/**

112. With the intentions of whispering a cautionary message in his ear_____**Y/**

113. However, my light-footedness sent tingling disturbances across his skin_____**Y/**

114. Without opening his eyes, he raised a hand_____**Y/**

115. And swatted_____**Y/**

116. And smashed down upon me_____**Y/**

117. Splattering my blood and body parts across his face_____**Y/**

118. He shot up out of bed_____**Y/**

119. Wiping pieces of the twitching insect off his cheek_____**Y/**

120. He proceeded to get dressed into his charcoal colored robe_____**Y/**

121. Mother Superior came knocking at his door_____**Y/**

122. She burst in—not waiting for him to respond_____**Y/**

123. She was concerned about the girl whom he'd been exorcising of a demon_____**Y/**

124. Mother Superior attempted to convince him_____**Y/**

125. To reevaluate the poor girl's situation_____**Y/**

126. The girl, an orphan, had a long depressing history of mental illness_____**Y/**

127. She'd been in and out of hospitals and mental institutions_____**Y/**

128. Diagnosed with schizophrenia in her early teens_____**Y/**

129. Her problems might have been resolved_____**Y/**

130. By stronger medications and more dedicated healthcare_____**Y/**

131. The arrogant young monk pushed Mother Superior aside_____**Y/**

132. Angered that she, his subordinate, would dare to challenge his acumen_____**Y/**

133. He held onto his conviction that a demon claimed the girl_____**Y/**

134. Whom he kept in isolation—locked away inside the room across the hall_____**Y/**

135. Whom he'd mounted, by thick ropes, to an upright wooden cross_____**Y/**

136. Whom he'd been depriving of all food and water for, at least, three days now_____**Y/**

137. Whom he'd soon find dead from dehydration_____**Y/**

138. And for whose death he'd serve a prison term of seven years_____**Y/**

139. Followed by a life of lonely and remorseful contemplation_____**Y/**

CIRCLE THE MOST APPLICABLE ANSWER:

I DON'T RECALL ANY OF THIS   =   **-1**

I REMEMBER IT ALL   =   **+1**

Synopsis of Statements

Indicative of a Shared Past Life Regression

Frass, Elytron / You

1. Long ago, I was known by white Johns as the Half-breed Hooker_____ **Y/**

2. Of Dunolly, Victoria_____ **Y/**

3. The once-lovechild of a tragic affair_____ **Y/**

4. And a dreamer inside of The Dreaming_____ **Y/**

5. Pray-Mantis, the totem, was partially with me_____ **Y/**

6. The World was a nightmare incarnate_____ **Y/**

7. The Dreaming was its antinomy_____ **Y/**

8. There I languished in wishes fulfilled_____ **Y/**

9. In The Dreaming I was the master of all pain and pleasure_____ **Y/**

10. Granted by way of auto-erotic asphyxiation_____ **Y/**

11. Men withheld their ejaculate to shower me in gold and shimmering riches_____ **Y/**

12. Their tongues flicked in and out on my command_____ **Y/**

13. Lapped the liquid sweetmeats of my pussy like a pack of well trained dogs_____ **Y/**

14. In The World I was strangled, raped, and robbed_____ **Y/**

15. By two faceless Johns in Tully's Brothel, where I worked_____ **Y/**

16. Pray-Mantis' body was splitting down the middle_____ **Y/**

17. Only one half in The Dreaming_____ **Y/**

18. The rest of him stayed in The World, on the opposite side of space and time_____ **Y/**

19. Half of myself was there also_____ **Y/**

20. Consented to dual penetration of Johns'_____**N/**

21. Welcomed their hands constricting my throat_____**N/**

22. Forfeited my money and possessions freely_____**N/**

23. Both of them were holding knives_____**Y/**

24. My assailants chopped me into thirds_____**Y/**

25. Pray-Mantis split itself into three segments_____**Y/**

26. I was transferred to the Land of My Ancestral Dead_____**Y/**

27. In the long gone body of my father_____**Y/**

28. In the month of July: in the year of 1891_____**Y/**

29. My father: a feather-weight of a John_____**Y/**

30. Strung up by the noose from the fan on the ceiling_____**Y/**

31. On top of a bed in the brothel, she lay under his dangling toes_____**Y/**

32. The Aboriginal girl; my teen mother at work, before I'd been conceived_____**Y/**

33. Contortion: her virtue_____**Y/**

34. Her mouth digging into her own moist black velvet_____**Y/**

35. Teeth and tongue burrowed deep in her pink canal_____**Y/**

36. As my father, I reckoned, *this is her greatest achievement*_____**Y/**

37. The display of raw talent combined with the pull of the noose triggered cum_____**Y/**

38. Triggered ecstasy_____**Y/**

39. She spread out—maw gaping—right below my dangling feet_____**Y/**

40. To catch the trickling liquid lunch_____**Y/**

41. Then contorted once again_____**Y/**

42. To hawk the mouthful of my load into her cervix_____**Y/**

43. I thought as my father: *this woman will be the bearer of my halfbreed daughter*_____**N/**

44. *To be raised and employed in this very brothel*_____**N/**

45. *An eventual victim of irony*_____**N/**

46. *Below this approximate spot where I currently hang*_____**N/**

47. In his mind I saw the foretelling of neither my fate nor conception_____**Y/**

48. His phallus was flooding with blood, cum, and bliss_____**Y/**

49. His whore spewed his seed into her womb_____**Y/**

50. And he was too gone to come off of the rope on his own_____**Y/**

51. Going this way was less harsh than the grit of the gold rush_____**Y/**

52. Scorched by Australia's blistering sun_____**Y/**

53. Soon he'd return to the goldfields to mine_____**N/**

54. The blood could not reach past the noose to his brain_____**Y/**

55. Complexion turned rosy to red, then violet to blue_____**Y/**

56. Flushed down to his toes_____**Y/**

57. Curled in then relaxed_____**Y/**

58. Gone numb, then gone-gone_____**Y/**

59. He left with a *POP* in his cervical spine_____**Y/**

60. We'd meet in the mouth of Pray-Mantis' claws_____**Y/**

61. Connecting The World and The Dreaming to the Land of Our Ancestral Dead_____**Y/**

62. My mother—held responsible for his death_____**Y/**

63. Was imprisoned for life after reaching full term_____**Y/**

CIRCLE THE MOST APPLICABLE ANSWER:

I DON'T RECALL ANY OF THIS   =   **-1**

I REMEMBER IT ALL   =   **+1**

Synopsis of Statements

Indicative of a Shared Past Life Regression

Frass, Elytron / You

1. Long ago, they labeled me a heathen woman_____**Y/**

2. Named Lasses Birgitta [wife of Lasse]_____**Y/**

3. A practitioner of necromancy and arthropodomancy_____**N/**

4. Communed with spirits of the dead_____**N/**

5. Commanded arthropods, found on the dead or near the dead, to carry out my will___**N/**

6. Resided on the island of Öland [part of Sweden], in Algutsrum_____**Y/**

7. The first woman to be executed as a sorceress in Sweden_____**Y/**

8. More than one hundred years before the witch hunts throughout Europe_____**Y/**

9. For my trial I was taken up to Kalmar Castle_____**Y/**

10. Where its secretary and my bailiff listened to my full confession_____**Y/**

11. Two men and I entered Kastlösa cemetery at midnight_____**Y/**

12. To reawaken a corpse from death_____**N/**

13. I encircled the graveyard's church three times_____**N/**

14. Blew into the keyhole of its door until it opened_____**N/**

15. So that we might procure a baptismal stole_____**N /**

16. To be placed on the corpse—aiding its revival_____**N/**

17. I attempted this on two occasions_____**N/**

18. Upon the second I managed to steal it_____**N/**

19. Encircled the church an additional three times against the sun_____**N/**

20. Renounced the Christian god and promised my soul to the Star of Morning_____ **N/**

21. The men who accompanied me were fined_____ **Y/**

22. But I was sentenced to death by decapitation_____ **Y/**

23. By the guillotine_____ **N /**

24. By axe_____ **Y/**

25. Swung down, passing through my lower jaw_____ **Y/**

26. Lower jaw: still attached to my neck afterwards_____ **Y/**

27. My consciousness stuck with my head_____ **Y/**

28. Which tumbled into the bucket below_____ **Y/**

29. Down through its spiraling bottomless hole_____ **Y/**

30. Bled into the cosmos, echoing_____ **Y/**

31. Redeaths of my futures and pasts_____ **Y/**

32. Engulfed by mantises swarming in aether_____ **Y/**

33. Whose six-legged legions latched onto my head in midflight_____ **Y/**

34. Their spiracles seethed queer gases and lights_____ **Y/**

35. Perceived as mere gases and lights_____ **N/**

36. Which manifested in forms of fairies and ghosts_____ **Y/**

37. Prepared for the Wilde Jagd_____ **Y/**

38. Together we crossed the obsidian skies_____ **Y/**

39. Ascended to earth once again_____ **Y/**

40. A veritable greenish inferno_____ **Y/**

41. A rainforest plagued abyss_____ **Y/**

42. The mantises set my head loose on the world _____ **Y/**

43. I was dropped from the air_____ **Y/**

44. Down through moist canopies_____ **Y/**

45. And onto the tip of a spear_____**Y/**

46. Wielded by an indigenous woman_____**Y/**

47. Who saw my appearance as an omen of war_____**Y/**

48. Cried out to her sisters and daughters_____**Y/**

49. It was June, 24, 1542_____**Y/**

50. The Spaniards set sail into the brackish and uncharted river nearby_____**Y/**

51. Francisco de Orellana raised up his sword_____**Y/**

52. Commanded his men to steer onward_____**Y/**

53. Hosts of radiant mantises, fairies, and ghosts could be seen through the trees_____**Y/**

54. They possessed native huntresses armed with arrows and bows_____**Y/**

55. Destroyed the armada_____**Y/**

56. Alas, de Orellana survived and escaped_____**Y/**

57. Returned to his homeland to warn of the Amazon horde_____**Y/**

58. And of that satanic place, he'd call Amazonas_____**Y/**

59. My head—still skewered by spear—was chucked into the Amazon river_____**Y/**

60. In the river I closed my eyes_____**Y/**

61. In the river I could sleep_____**Y/**

CIRCLE THE MOST APPLICABLE ANSWER:

I DON'T RECALL ANY OF THIS   =   **-1**

I REMEMBER IT ALL   =   **+1**

Synopsis of Statements

Indicative of a Shared Past Life Regression

Frass, Elytron / You

1. Long ago, I was someone else_____ **Y/**

2. My name was Tim [Peters]_____ **?/**

3. My name was [Tim] Peters_____ **?/**

4. Born July, 4, 1934_____ **Y/**

5. Too young to be drafted by the time of the Second World War_____ **Y/**

6. Had I been of ripe age to be drafted, they would have rejected me anyhow_____ **Y/**

7. Due to a childhood injury_____ **Y/**

8. Acquired while running with scissors in primary school_____ **Y/**

9. Resulting in the total loss of sight in my right eye_____ **Y/**

10. I had two other siblings_____ **N/**

11. Mother and father were dead_____ **N/**

12. We lived in a lake house together_____ **Y/**

13. By Sebasticook Lake_____ **Y/**

14. In Penobscot County, Maine_____ **Y/**

15. At eighteen years old,　I spent my last summer there_____ **Y/**

16. Prepared to leave home for college in Autumn_____ **Y/**

17. I earned a full scholarship to the University of Nebraska-Lincoln_____ **Y/**

18. Planned to pursue a degree in the field of entomology_____ **Y/**

19. Before finishing high school, I'd already been published in a scientific journal_____ **Y/**

20. Wrote on a species of stonefly_____ **Y/**

21. I'd discovered and named it_____**Y/**

22. It was endemic to Maine_____**Y/**

23. Became pen pals with countless professors and researches_____**Y/**

24. I was an extremely sociable teen_____**N/**

25. However, if someone got me going on the topic of insects, I wouldn't shut up_____**Y/**

26. My perfectly functioning left eye: always focused upon their intricate world_____**Y/**

27. Their hardworking and cutthroat societies mirrored our own_____**Y/**

28. During what should've been my last week at home, I received a curious parcel_____**Y/**

29. With a return address on it_____**N/**

30. Its contents were a pin and an unmounted species of mantis_____**Y/**

31. And, also, three identification labels_____**Y/**

32. These things were packaged with care_____**N/**

33. The mantis, for instance, was missing its head_____**Y/**

34. The three small rectangular labels had clear writings on them_____**Y/**

35. Meant to be placed under the specimen and pinned altogether_____**Y/**

36. The text on the labels was fading, and the index card stock looked very old_____**Y/**

37. There were no other contents other than these_____**Y/**

38. I examined the labels_____**Y/**

39. The first one read: IN: Cova da Iria

                                                          Fatima, Portugal

                                                          October, 13, 1917_____**Y/**

40. The second read: Found alive, headless, in a field

                              Among a crowd of Portuguese

                              During the Miracle of the Sun_____**Y/**

41. And the last/final label read: ID: *Mantis* sp., most likely either

                              chhinnamastayai or *chinnamundayai*_____**Y/**

42. I stacked these curious labels in order—first to last_____**Y/**

43. Tucked them under the underside of the specimen_____**Y/**

44. Pushed the pin into its upper abdomen, just below where it borders the thorax_____**Y/**

45. The pin started to vibrate between my forefingers and thumb_____**Y/**

46. My fingertips blistered around it_____**Y/**

47. Giving off a sulfuric odor_____**Y/**

48. *Less like burning flesh...more like rotten eggs*_____**Y/**

49. An unbearable humming rattled my skull_____**Y/**

50. My hands cupped over my ears_____**Y/**

51. An intensified heat acutely spread through my insides_____**Y/**

52. My sex organs burned like never before_____**Y/**

53. Overcome by a nerve wracking surge of bewildering déja vu_____**Y/**

54. Which faded too fast from my mind before I could place it in time_____**Y/**

55. I immediately told my family about this_____**N/**

56. I quietly suffered from nausea and headaches for days_____**Y/**

57. My genitals blistered as if I'd contracted an STD_____**Y/**

58. An uncanny sense of nostalgia pervaded my feelings and thoughts_____**Y/**

59. The vaguest transgression that could have trouble me into my grave_____**Y/**

60. Finally, I saw a doctor_____**Y/**

61. Named Steven [Ianson]_____N/

62. Named [Steven] Ianson_____N/

63. An astute hypnotist_____Y/

64. Who lulled me with his swinging watch and suggestions_____Y/

65. Into a state of awareness wherein I remembered a lucid account_____Y/

66. Of my abduction by alien sex fiends_____N/

67. Of a life reaching back to the days of antiquity_____Y/

68. Born from a people who came from the mountains and knew nothing of grain_____Y/

69. Westerners of the Near East_____Y/

70. We were herdsman and mercenaries_____Y/

71. Who brought bulls and goats to the eastern Near East_____Y/

72. Oblations for the goddess Inanna_____Y/

73. We infiltrated its cities like shadows_____Y/

74. Assimilated into its culture_____Y/

75. Usurped and united the reign of its lands_____Y/

76. Our Amorite king ushered us into a golden age under his rule_____Y/

77. He was my father_____Y/

78. And I was prince and heir to Mesopotamia_____Y/

79. Named Samsu-iluna_____?/

80. When I became king I sat on my throne in palatial opulence_____N/

81. Met with nothing but conflict once handed the crown_____Y/

82. My strategic advisor suggested I visit Inanna's most sacred temple_____Y/

83. Where the Goddess' priestess copulated with kings for good omens_____Y/

84. So, I arranged for a visit with her_____Y/

85. My wife was possessive and jealous_____Y/

86. Her name was Ashlutum_____Y/

87. She begged to accompany me_____Y/

88. I allowed her to do so_____N/

89. She swore that she'd get her revenge_____Y/

90. I temporarily placed my advisor in charge of the throne_____Y/

91. As Elam and Assyria planned to revolt_____Y/

92. Inanna's temple was located in the heart our capital, Babylon_____Y/

93. North of the ziggurat_____N/

94. I was escorted by by one of my most loyal guards_____Y/

95. Who wasn't permitted to pass through the temple's gold doors_____Y/

96. The priestess was there to lead me inside_____Y/

97. She was dressed in a sheer rose colored gown and a veil_____Y/

98. Stripped herself bare as she led me through torchlit hallways of stone_____Y/

99. She stunned me with her preponderant beauty and curves_____Y/

100. I wanted to force her onto the floor and ravish her ass and womb_____Y/

101. Yet, I continued to follow_____Y/

102. Determined to conquer her body at a more appropriate time_____Y/

103. My arrogance was proportionate to my inherited affluence_____Y/

104. The shepherd-god, Dumuzi, was arrogant too_____Y/

105. His arrogance led to defilement, death, and rebirth_____Y/

106. I was just like Dumuzi_____Y/

107. I was brought to a room with a circular opening in its domed roof_____Y/

108. Potent sunrays beamed onto a central altar_____Y/

109. Excessively heated its surface of gold_____Y/

110. It was rumored that one could fry ibis eggs on it throughout the day_____Y/

111. This was where, I was told, virgin infants were sacrificed to Inanna_____ **Y/**

112. Baked by the refraction of sun in Her eye—staring down, up in heaven_____ **Y/**

113. This was also the table upon where we'd consummate ritual sex_____ **Y/**

114. Where Inanna—half woman, half beast—could spy from the hole in the dome____ **Y/**

115. We'd perform this at nightfall—to avoid scorching our hides_____ **Y/**

116. I was shown into an adjacent bedchamber_____ **Y/**

117. Urged to rest up_____ **Y/**

118. She'd come back for me when it was time_____ **Y/**

119. I remained awake—fantasizing about what I thought would transpire_____ **Y/**

120. I'd roleplay as God of the Shepherds, Dumuzi_____ **Y/**

121. As Dumuzi I would mount Inanna, embodied by the priestess_____ **Y/**

122. I awaited the sacred whore— my eyes: fixed on the doorway_____ **Y/**

123. She returned when the ritual neared_____ **Y/**

124. She called me Dumuzi_____ **Y/**

125. Reintroduced herself as Inanna_____ **N/**

126. As Inanna's top servant, Ninshubur_____ **Y/**

127. I was hushed into silence before I could question_____ **Y/**

128. She got behind me and covered my eyes_____ **Y/**

129. Ninshubur prodded me into the room of my mystery bride_____ **Y/**

130. Where Ashlutum, my wife, splayed nude on the altar_____ **Y/**

131. Taking the role of primordial half-god/half-monster_____ **Y/**

132. Who purred like a kitten_____ **Y/**

133. And spread out her legs like a mantis' claws_____ **Y/**

134. I was forced to kneel down by her sex_____ **Y/**

135. My back and my ass were beading with sweat_____ **Y/**

136. Her servant, behind me, clutched chunks of my hair_____**Y/**

137. From the nape of my neck to my tailbone_____**Y/**

138. Ninshubur's thumb traced down my spine_____**Y/**

139. And then pressed it into my underworld_____**Y/**

140. I registered blissful intrusion_____**Y/**

141. As her other hand pushed my face into Inanna-Ashlutum's gash_____**Y/**

142. My wife-goddess widened her gaping abyss_____**Y/**

143. Swallowed my head_____**Y/**

144. I was held in her chasm for hundreds of years_____**Y/**

145. Elam and Assyria succeeded_____**Y/**

146. Hittite, Hurrian, and Kassite armies invaded_____**Y/**

147. My Babylon crumbled_____**Y/**

148. Just like Dumuzi, I was defiled and slain_____**Y/**

149. And, then, born once again_____**Y/**

150. In 1917, I was a thirty-three year old–living in Fátima, Portugal_____**Y/**

151. My name was Francisco [Marto]_____**N/**

152. My name was [Fransico] Marto_____**N/**

153. I had a wife named Jacinta_____**Y/**

154. Who's lover, Artur, remained my best friend_____**Y/**

155. Artur was a physicist_____**Y/**

156. I was a botanist_____**Y/**

157. Jacinta was an éminence grise_____**Y/**

158. She was not an academic per se_____**Y/**

159. Academia was her hunting ground_____**Y/**

160. She was a fastidious heterotroph_____**Y/**

161. An obligate eater of men_____**Y/**

162. A love triangle orchestrator_____**Y/**

163. Once, I was her lover_____**Y/**

164. At that time, she was still married to a passive entomologist, José de Almeida_____**Y/**

165. As soon as I put a new ring on her finger my days as her lover were numbered____**Y/**

166. Sometime in May, 1917, Artur was evicted from his residence_____**Y/**

167. He reached out to us for help_____**Y/**

168. We welcomed him into our home_____**Y/**

169. Within that very month, three indigo children were visited_____**Y/**

170. By apparitions of peculiar light_____**Y/**

171. Which collectively called themselves, 'Lady of Fátima'_____**Y/**

172. And had access to memory banks of our futures and pasts_____**Y/**

173. The indigo children foresaw their own deaths_____**Y/**

174. Promised the end of World War I_____**Y/**

175. And prophesized the majestic return of the Lady of Fátima_____**Y/**

176. On October, 13, 1917, I stood with a crowd in a field at Cova da Iria_____**Y/**

177. Near Fátima, Portugal_____**Y/**

178. There was over thirty thousand of us there to bear witness_____**Y/**

179. I was very religious_____**N/**

180. Yet, I wanted to see what everyone else had already believed_____**Y/**

181. The sun went from orange to cherry red, until finally, it settled into violet_____**Y/**

182. Unfixed itself from the sky_____**Y/**

183. Zigzagged down and across the horizon line_____**Y/**

184. I broke out in chills and gooseflesh_____**Y/**

185. And awed at the UFO_____**Y/**

186. Which inflicted me with an acute case of conjunctivitis_____ **Y/**

187. Even as the lights seared my sclera I couldn't bother blinking_____ **Y/**

188. Only looking away once feeling the presence of something below_____ **Y/**

189. It scuttled over my foot_____ **Y/**

190. An astoundingly vital yet headless insect_____ **Y/**

191. Its forelegs reached upward and folded as if engaging in prayer_____ **Y/**

192. The sun fixed itself back into place_____ **Y/**

193. The crowd lingered—expecting an encore_____ **Y/**

194. I stowed the miraculous insect in my pocket_____ **Y/**

195. Then navigated a path through the crowd_____ **Y/**

196. I stopped at the post office before going home_____ **Y/**

197. I was no expert on insects_____ **Y/**

198. But by way of botany I knew that this creature was some type of mantis_____ **Y/**

199. Sealed it up in a box and shipped it to the one person I'd known in the field_____ **Y/**

200. José de Almeida_____ **Y/**

201. I arrived to my seemingly empty house bursting with wonderful feelings_____ **Y/**

202. Excited to share my experience with Jacinta and Artur_____ **Y/**

203. This was a rare departure from my typically nonplused disposition_____ **Y/**

204. Interrupted by a dysrhythmic creaking of bedsprings_____ **Y/**

205. Hardly audible moaning_____ **Y/**

206. The percussion of flesh slapping flesh_____ **Y/**

207. I snuck up to my and Jacinta's closed bedroom door_____ **Y/**

208. Peered into the keyhole_____ **Y/**

209. Artur was belly-up_____ **Y/**

210. Jacinta stood over him_____ **Y/**

211. His cock was throbbing and erect_____**Y/**

212. As was mine_____**Y/**

213. We were two cadavers waiting to be buried in a hole_____**Y/**

214. She bent her knees and sat upon his face_____**Y/**

215. I touched myself as she began to ride_____**Y/**

216. His head was eagerly devoured by her cunt_____**Y/**

217. Jacinta's upper body stretched along his lower half_____**Y/**

218. Her mouth closed over his pulsating penis_____**Y/**

219. She'd taken all of him inside_____**Y/**

220. Underneath her, his entire shape was disappearing_____**Y/**

221. Everything that Artur was dissolved_____**Y/**

222. A man eradicated by the sex of his new lover_____**Y/**

223. It terrified as much as it had titillated him_____**Y/**

224. I knew this because we'd talk about it afterward over cigarettes and brunch_____**Y/**

225. Just as I had once relayed this sort of information to José_____**Y/**

226. I became excited by the fear of ceasing to exist_____**Y/**

227. My role as Jacinta's spouse receded_____**Y/**

228. On the other side, beyond hypnosis, I was catatonic_____**Y/**

229. My doctor tried to coax me out of my regression_____**Y/**

230. He snapped his fingers_____**Y/**

231. Nudged me, shook me—calling out my name_____**Y/**

232. But I would not respond_____**Y/**

233. No longer the person I was at the time I'd gone under hypnosis_____**Y/**

234. All entrances/exits were leads to extinctions_____**Y/**

CIRCLE THE MOST APPLICABLE ANSWER:

I DON'T RECALL ANY OF THIS   =   **-1**

I REMEMBER IT ALL   =   **+1**

Synopsis of Statements

Indicative of a Shared Past Life Regression

Frass, Elytron / You

1. Long ago, my name was Ngawang Tenzin Rinpoche_____ **Y/**
2. I was the wife of a polyandrous marriage_____ **Y/**
3. To my lover and his brother_____ **Y/**
4. Who mutually owned land within the Yarlung River Valley_____ **Y/**
5. Which was purchased by the earnings of a lucky gambling streak_____ **Y/**
6. At the height of the Tibetan Empire, circa 640 AD_____ **Y/**
7. We prospered with a plethora of racing horses and a goji berry farm_____ **Y/**
8. My lover and his brother sandwiched me with short-lived coitus every night_____ **Y/**
9. Afterward we would routinely spoon to ease ourselves to sleep_____ **Y/**
10. They'd often ask me to recount the stories of my previous life_____ **Y/**
11. Fascinated by my vivid memories as one lowly praying mantis_____ **Y/**
12. Who's self-decapitation altered patterns of her karmic wheel_____ **Y/**
13. Causing her rebirth into the human race_____ **Y/**
14. My husbands always stayed awake until the end_____ **Y/**
15. However, on one night in particular, they stopped me in the middle of my tale_____ **Y/**
16. Their heads hung low with something weighing heavy on their minds_____ **Y/**
17. They'd lost a string of bets on risky horses_____ **Y/**
18. Accrued a hefty debt_____ **Y/**
19. Much greater than our rural fortunes_____ **Y/**
20. A debt collector was on his way from China_____ **Y/**

21. Arriving noon, tomorrow_____**Y/**

22. He'd want no less than an organ or a limb if we failed to pay in full_____**Y/**

23. My lover's brother suggested I give up my head_____**Y/**

24. My lover disagreed_____**N/**

25. In his opinion, if my remembrances were true, I wouldn't lose my head in vain_____**Y/**

26. He hypothesized, as like before, that I'd ascend_____**Y/**

27. Moreover, his brother argued, a selfless act as this would grant me Buddhahood____**Y/**

28. I thought about it for a second but withheld my answer for the time_____**Y/**

29. I waited until my husbands were asleep_____**Y/**

30. Slipped out through the door with stallion furs to keep me warm_____**Y/**

31. I hung around our land until the afternoon_____**Y/**

32. Saw the debt collector leaving with red hands_____**Y/**

33. I went back into the house once he had gone_____**Y/**

34. The living room was blood-drenched_____**Y/**

35. I ran over to my husbands—doubled over in their matching chairs_____**Y/**

36. Their bloodied hands cupped over ruined and gored groins_____**Y/**

37. Before my lover passed away he pointed to a box left on the table by our guest_____**Y/**

38. *Something to remember me and my brother by,* he said_____**Y/**

39. The box was plated with gold foil_____**Y/**

40. As I opened it I was a tad confused_____**Y/**

41. Inside were two small bloodied objects_____**Y/**

42. Which, more or less, resembled Chinese eggplants_____**Y/**

43. Shriveled Chinese eggplants, I should add_____**Y/**

44. I put them in a planting pot and buried them in soil_____**Y/**

45. My lover and his brother rotted in the following weeks within our home_____**Y/**

46. I couldn't let myself be bothered with that mess_____**Y/**

47. I was far too busy watching Chinese eggplants grow_____**Y/**

48. I plucked them when they ripened—long and firm and full of girth_____**Y/**

49. These two felt fuller in my ass and cunt than those I'd had before_____**Y/**

50. I slid them in and out to make me cum_____**Y/**

51. They spread peculiar fragrances throughout my body's core_____**Y/**

52. Until I tasted notes of Chinese eggplant on my tongue_____**Y/**

53. I pulled them out in order to examine them again_____**Y/**

54. I took notice of their false realities as (so called) eggplants_____**Y/**

55. False images of eggplants that impressed themselves upon the phalli underneath___**Y/**

56. False phalli which were superimpositions over veins_____**Y/**

57. Superimpositions over arteries and blood-filled spaces_____**Y/**

58. Which were also superimpositions over cells and molecules and so on_____**Y/**

59. The same things could be said about my head_____   _____**Y/**

60. In the realm of senses there was nothing but illusions_____**Y/**

61. Devoid of existential absoluteness_____**Y/**

62. My head was not a head, and it was neither here nor there_____**Y/**

CIRCLE THE MOST APPLICABLE ANSWER:

I DON'T RECALL ANY OF THIS   =   -1

I REMEMBER IT ALL   =   +1

GRAND TOTAL SCORES:

IF **+9** OR **GREATER**, GO TO PAGE **103**

IF **+8** OR **LESS** (EXCLUDING ZERO), GOT TO PAGE **87**

IF **ZERO** OR **NONPARTICIPATING**, GO TO PAGE **81**

CUM-COATED THORAX

WHETHER MANTISES ARE CONDUITS BETWEEN THE ENTITIES AND REGIONS WHICH
CONTINUE TO BE HINTED AT THROUGHOUT THE AGES OR PERCEPTIVE ILLUSIONISTS THAT
MANIFEST A TEMPORARY MIRROR TO OUR OWN IMAGINATION REMAINS UNKNOWABLE

Glyph	Value	Glyph	Value	Glyph	Value
	A1		J10		S19
	B2		K11		T20
	C3		L12		U21
	D4		M13		V22
	E5		N14		W23
	F6		O15		X24
	G7		P16		Y25
	H8		Q17		Z26
	I9		R18		SPACE/END 27

*COMPILED FROM ROSWELL, RENDLESHAM, UTSURO-BUNE UFO SITES

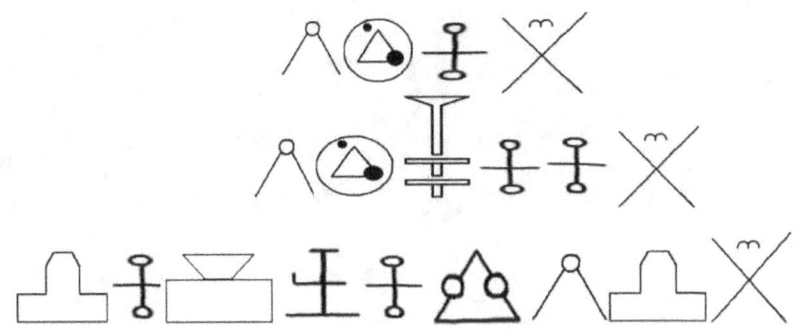

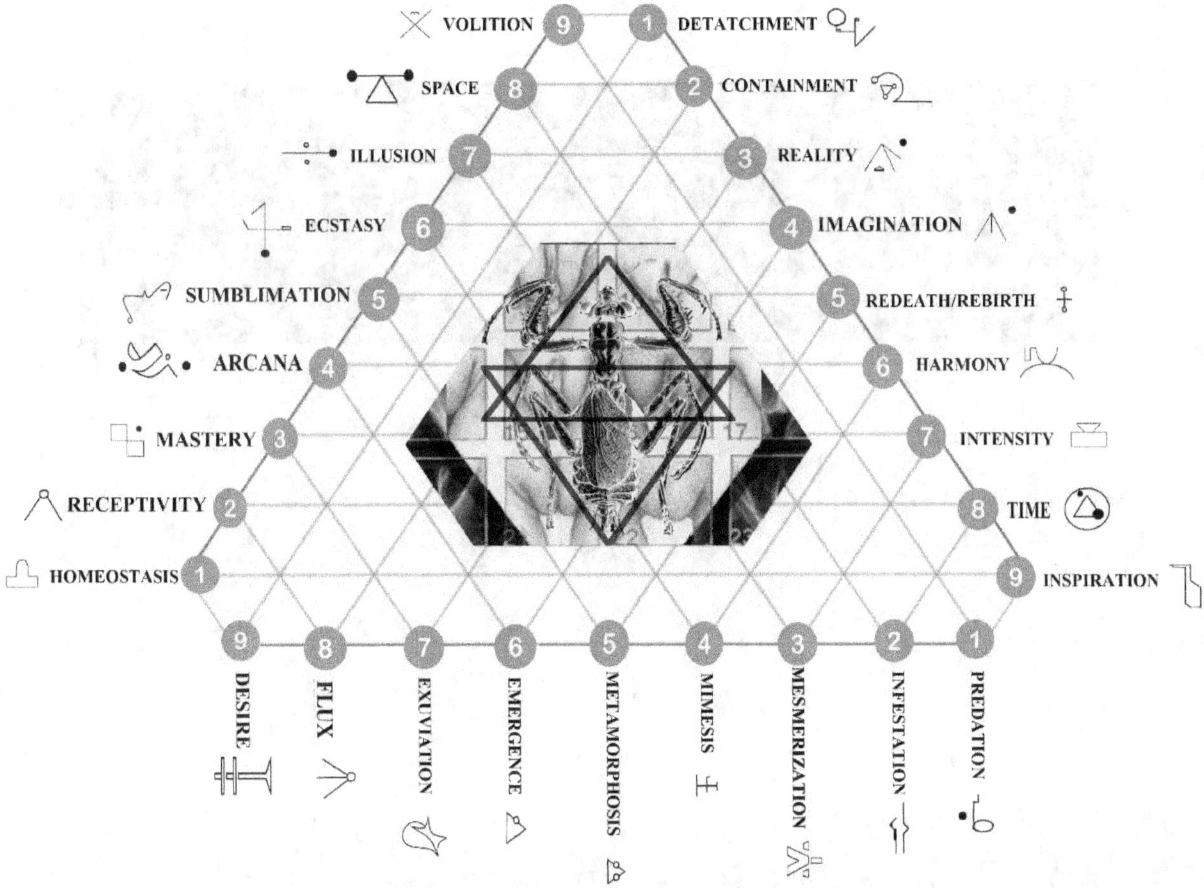

VOLITION 9   1 DETATCHMENT

SPACE 8   2 CONTAINMENT

ILLUSION 7   3 REALITY

ECSTASY 6   4 IMAGINATION

SUMBLIMATION 5   5 REDEATH/REBIRTH

ARCANA 4   6 HARMONY

MASTERY 3   7 INTENSITY

RECEPTIVITY 2   8 TIME

HOMEOSTASIS 1   9 INSPIRATION

9 8 7 6 5 4 3 2 1

DESIRE

FLUX

EXUVIATION

EMERGENCE

METAMORPHOSIS

MIMESIS

MESMERIZATION

INFESTATION

PREDATION

HEAD OVER TO...

HEAD, ON
PAGE 109

PISS-COATED THORAX

"IN ALL...

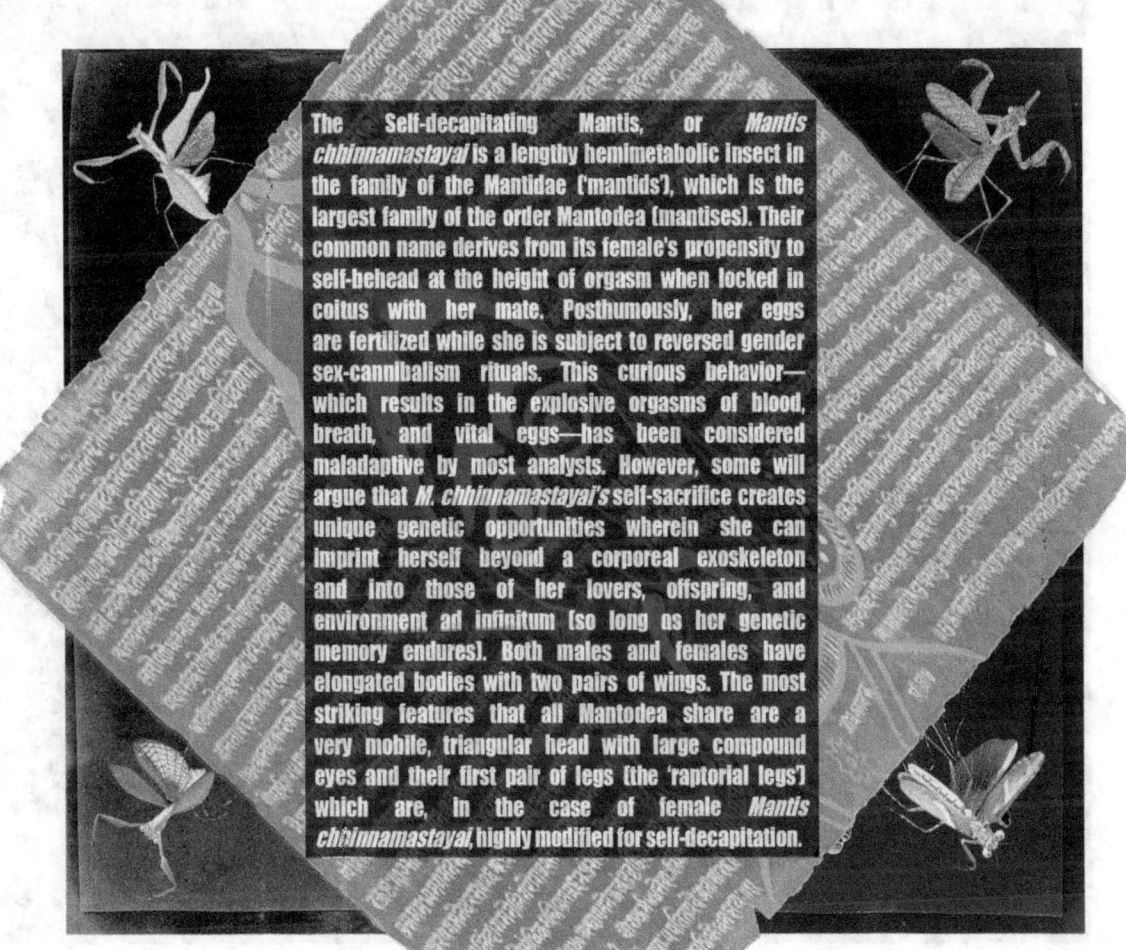

The Self-decapitating Mantis, or *Mantis chhinnamastayai* is a lengthy hemimetabolic insect in the family of the Mantidae ('mantids'), which is the largest family of the order Mantodea (mantises). Their common name derives from its female's propensity to self-behead at the height of orgasm when locked in coitus with her mate. Posthumously, her eggs are fertilized while she is subject to reversed gender sex-cannibalism rituals. This curious behavior—which results in the explosive orgasms of blood, breath, and vital eggs—has been considered maladaptive by most analysts. However, some will argue that *M. chhinnamastayai's* self-sacrifice creates unique genetic opportunities wherein she can imprint herself beyond a corporeal exoskeleton and into those of her lovers, offspring, and environment ad infinitum (so long as her genetic memory endures). Both males and females have elongated bodies with two pairs of wings. The most striking features that all Mantodea share are a very mobile, triangular head with large compound eyes and their first pair of legs (the 'raptorial legs') which are, in the case of female *Mantis chhinnamastayai*, highly modified for self-decapitation.

...OF THEM...

...ONE SEES...

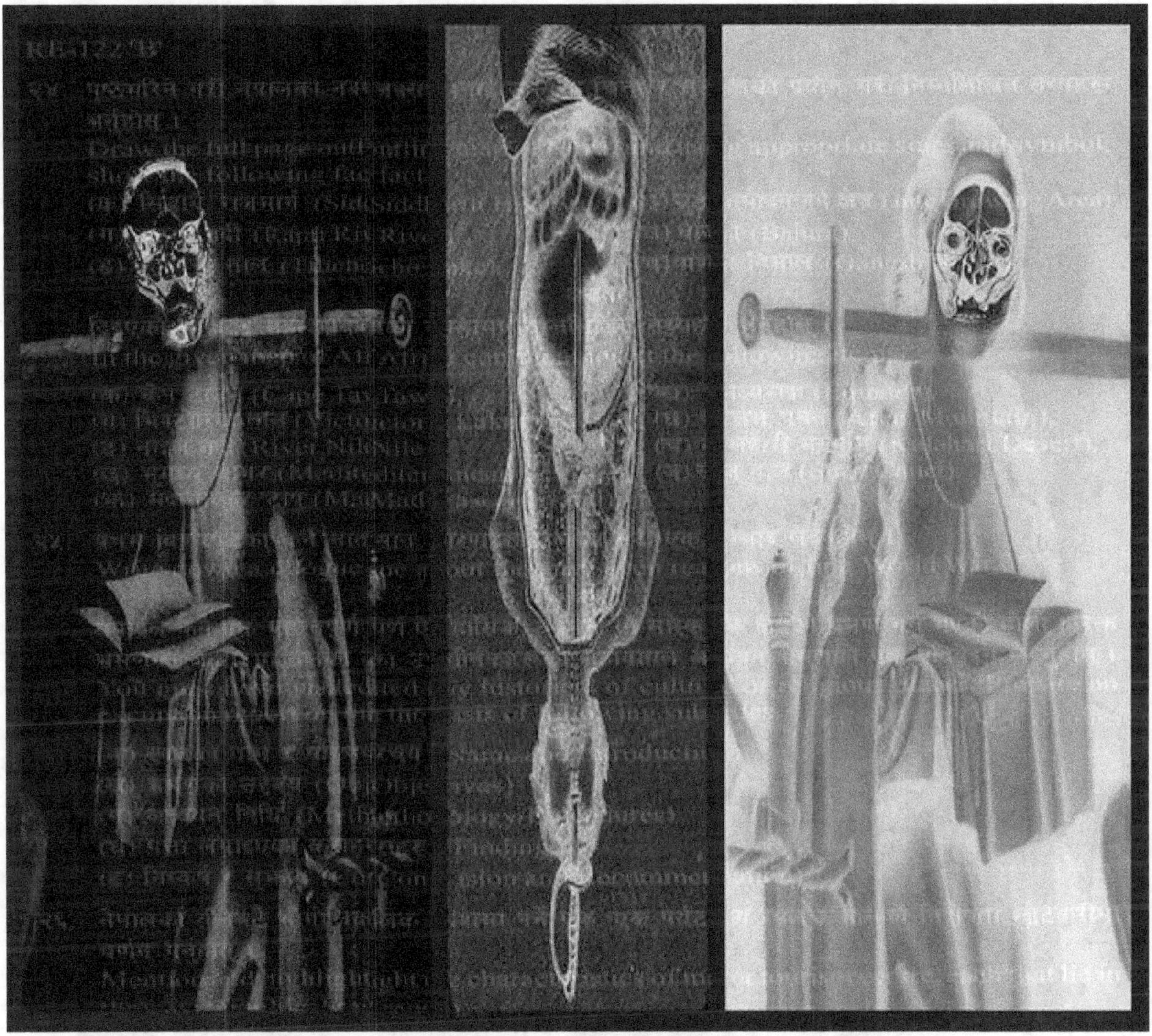

...INTENTIONAL...

...ARTIFACE; ONE...

...SEES THAT...

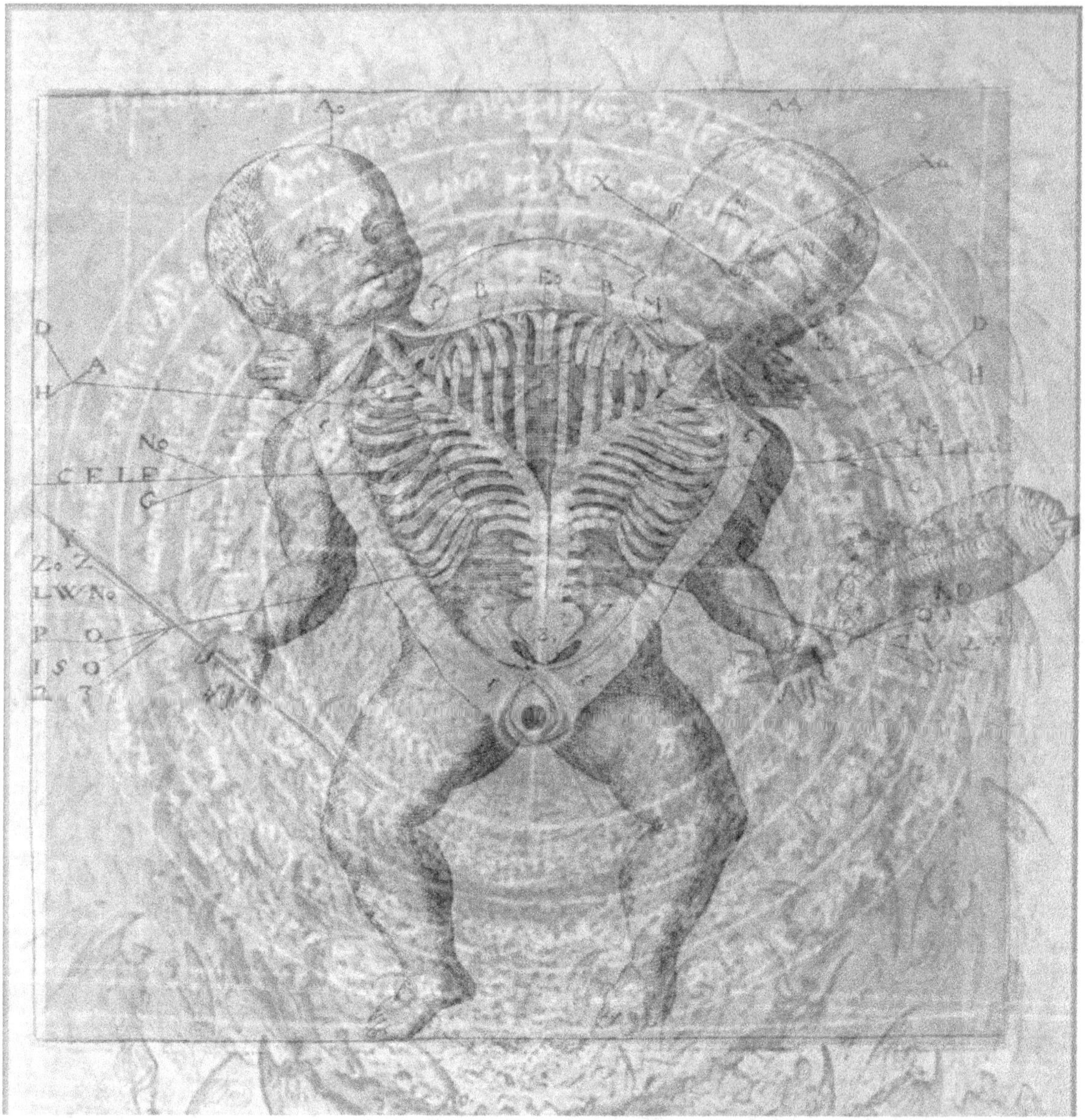

... [ELYTRON FRASS]...

...IS NOT...

...IN EARNEST, BUT...

...THAT HE...

...IS PLAYING...

The Self-beheading Mantis, or *Mantis chinnamundayai* is an insect whose common name derives from its female's tendency to self-decapitate in spite of courtship. Her total resignation as an ambush predator leaves little room for speculating *M. chinnamundayai's* karmic detachment from her place in insectkind. If the creature's goal is to obliterate its species, then her dwindling numbers are a necessary means to that extinction. It could be said that she is also an imagined construct of a flawed taxonomy which ultimately can't exist because each insect in the family of the Mantidae ('mantids'), which is the largest family of the order Mantodea (mantises) cannot exist as something independent from its genus (Mantis) which is void without its family (Mantidea) which could not define itself without inclusion of its order (Mantodae) which is a component of a superorder (Dictyoptera) which itself is a derivative of class (Insecta) which is entirely dependent upon an overarching phylum (Arthropoda) which branches from its kingdom (Animalia) born from a domain which, by design, falls short of classifying pseudo-living things, therefore, invalidating the apparent truths of taxonomic rank and rendering the labels empty of their inelastic meanings.

...WITH WORDS."

-REPURPOSED QUOTE OF SOME DEAD WRITER

HEAD OVER TO...

HEAD, ON PAGE 109

BLOOD-COATED THORAX

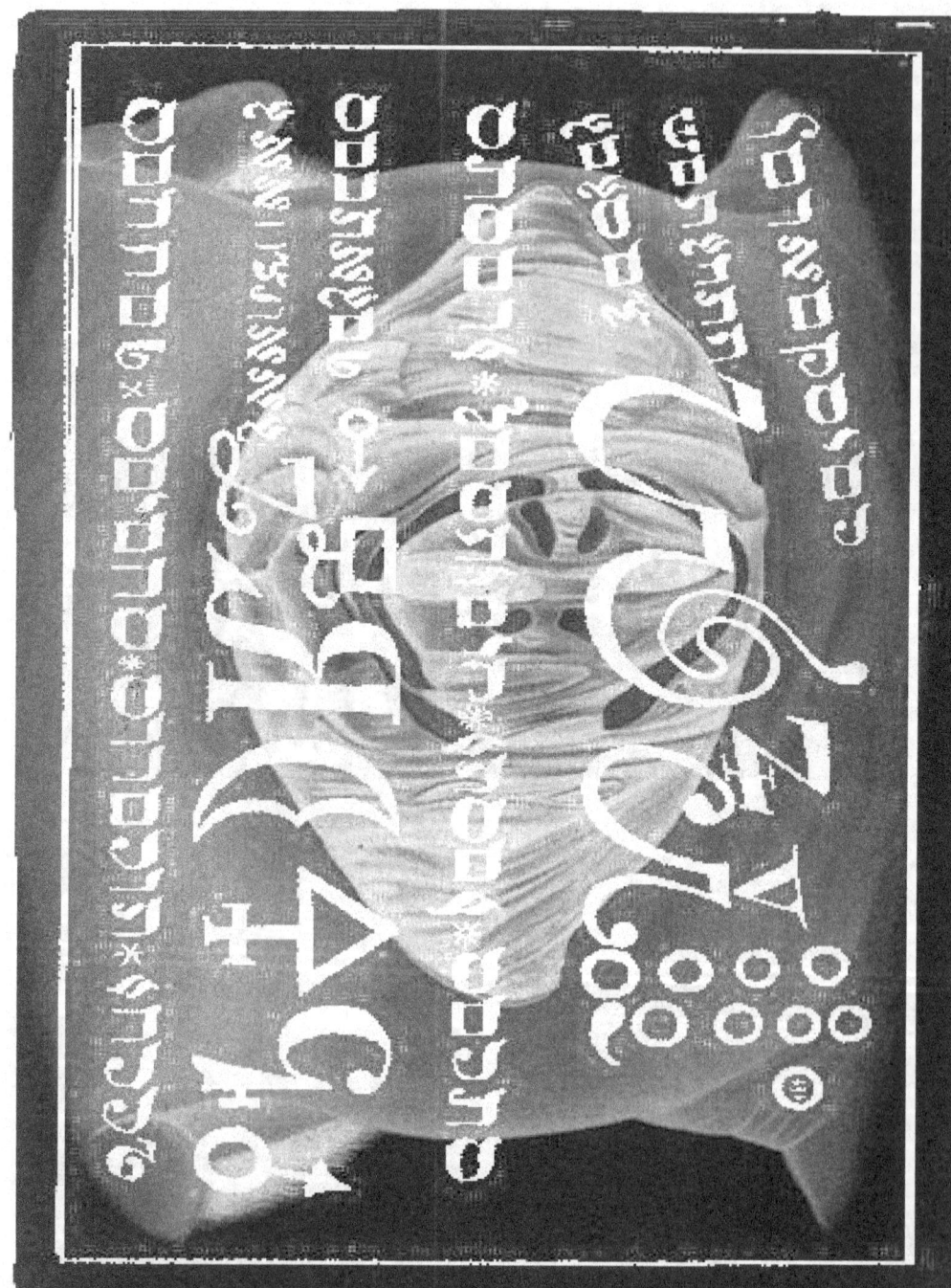

Quorum Psychiatric Associates, Medical Progress Note

Cercus Comb, MD
Psychiatrist

Next Appt: Day: Date: Time: Location/Room: **11**

MR #: ████████, DOB: 03/16/1984
Client: Frass, Elytron
Medicare #: ████████
Date: 7/27/2017

Physician	Activity	Recipients			
Dr. Comb	F/U	☒ Ct ☐ Ct & collaterals ☐ Ct & family ☐ Ct, collaterals, & family			

Client progress since last clinic visit: _____ Ct believes that his memories reach back thousands of years and span the world over. Today he expressed longing for whom he refers to as his "bifurcated self," or someone, somewhere, on this planet who mirrors his exact emotions, memories, and experiences. When asked about how he plans to go about seeking this doppelganger Ct stated, "I'm currently working on a book to aid my search; when it's complete I plan to mail it out to however many random households full of however many random persons until it finds one who will complete me." Worried that I'd been entertaining his delusions, I diverted with another question—asking him if writing was his source of income. However his reaction to this was surprisingly defensive. Before Ct abruptly cut our session short, he demanded copies of his psychiatric records thus far. And on his way out, he threatened, "You best not sabotage my monthly food stamps and my social security money—OR ELSE...!" I'm more concerned that Ct will just permanently discontinue Tx.

MSE: ☐ No Change   ☐ Change, as noted below:

Appearance	☐ Groomed	☐ Makeup	☐ Unkempt	☐ Body Odor	☒ Unusual	☐ Bizarre
Attitude	☐ Cooperative	☐ Guarded	☒ Uncooperative	☐ Hostile	☐ Over Friendly	
Motor Activity	☐ Calm	☒ Hyperactive	☒ Agitated	☐ Hypoactive	☐ Disorganized	☐ Rigid
Mood	☐ Normal	☐ Depressed	☒ Dysphoric	☐ Anxious	☐ Elevated	☐ Irritable
Affect	☐ Appropriate	☐ Inappropriate	☒ Labile	☐ Constricted	☐ Flat	☐ Blunted
Speech	☒ Normal	☐ Halting	☐ Pressured	☐ Slurred	☐ Incoherent	☐ Paucity
Thought Process	☐ Intact	☐ Tangential	☒ Flight of Ideas	☐ LOA	☐ Circumstantial	☐ Random
Thought Content	☐ Normal	☐ Halluc:Aud/Vis	☐ Tactile/Olfactory	☐ Del:Susp	☐ Persecutory	☒ Grandiose
Cognitive	☒ Alert	☐ Drowsy	Oriented: ☐ Person ☐ Place		☐ Time	☐ Situation

Client Report of Suicidal Ideation: Y ☐ N ☒   Homicidal Ideation: Y ☐ N ☒   Intent: Y ☐ N ☒   Plan: Y ☐ N ☒

MSE Narrative: While Ct denies intent/plans to harm self/others, his frequent flights of ideas are full of morbid, erotic-grotesque content—most notably his intermittent anecdotes on the improbabilities of self-decapitation. Moreover, his intermittent disorientation to time and place is magnified when he is at his most dysphoric—often stating, "I don't belong in this body. I am a mere half of myself."

Fig. 23.

HEAD OVER TO...

HEAD, ON PAGE 109

HEAD

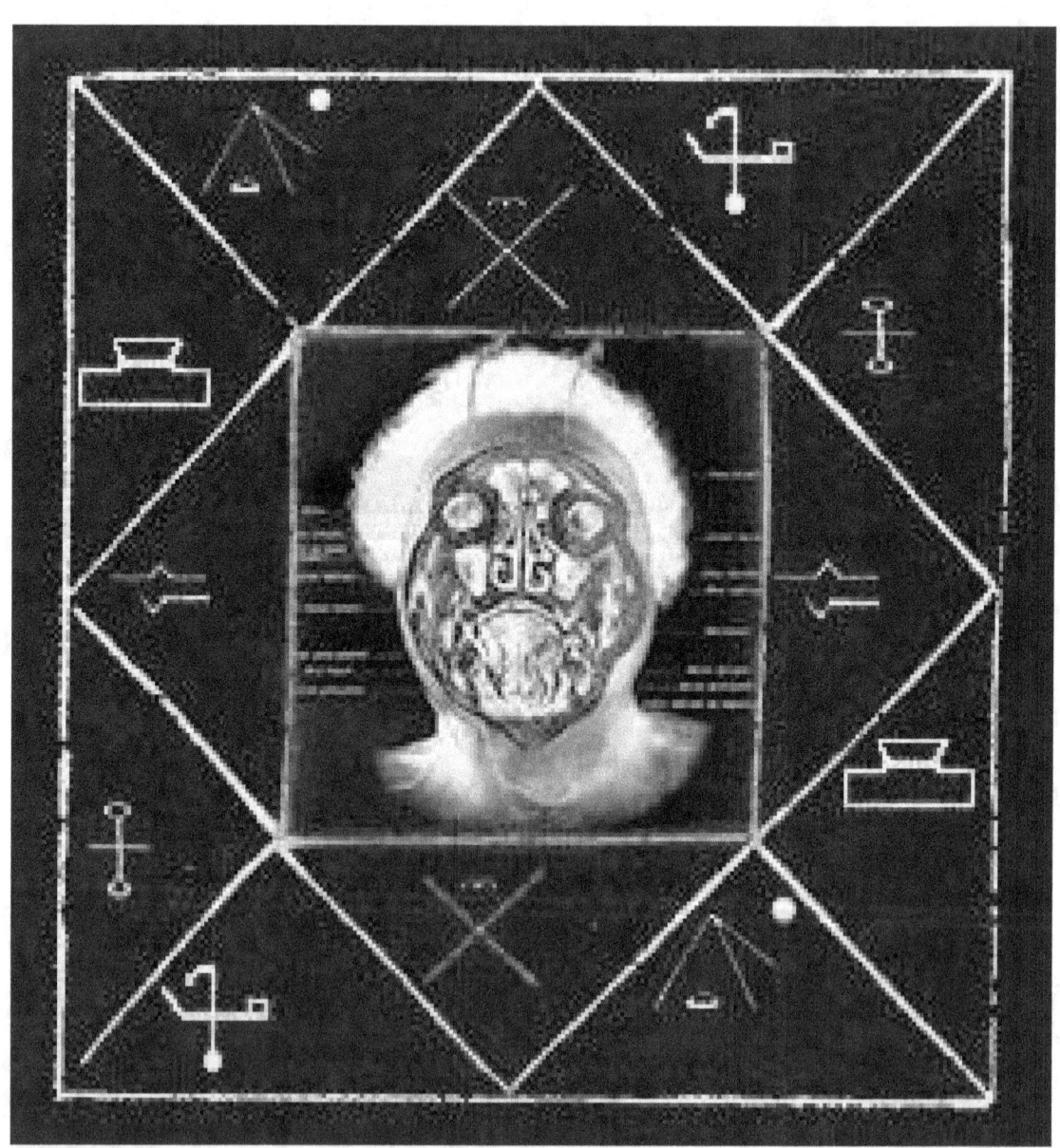

ONLY USE THIS SEAL TO HELP

RETURN TO THE FRONT PAGE

OR MOVE ONWARD TO THE NEXT

FORGET WHAT YOU HAVE READ

OH AW(E)FUL ONE PLEASE PREY UPON ME

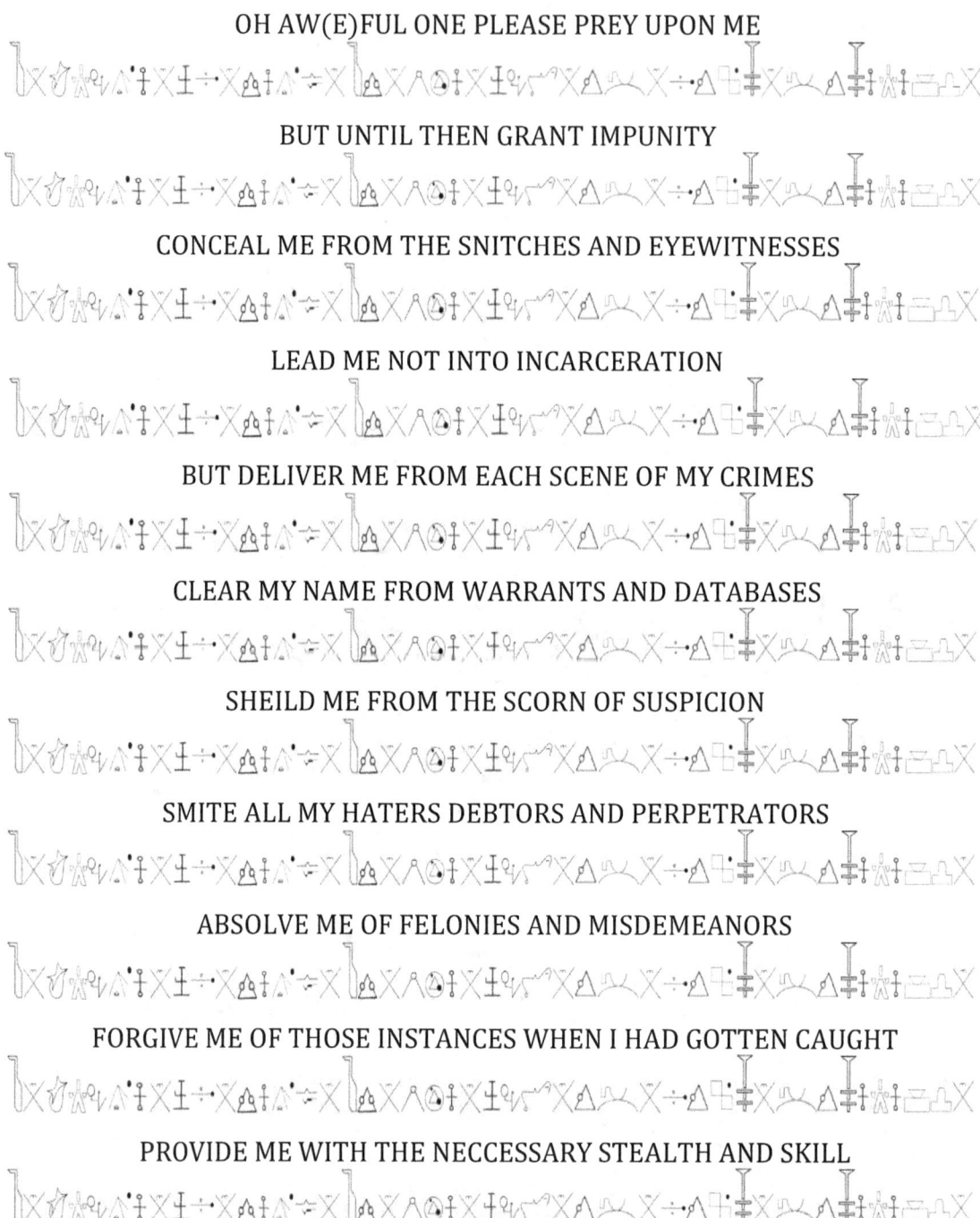

BUT UNTIL THEN GRANT IMPUNITY

CONCEAL ME FROM THE SNITCHES AND EYEWITNESSES

LEAD ME NOT INTO INCARCERATION

BUT DELIVER ME FROM EACH SCENE OF MY CRIMES

CLEAR MY NAME FROM WARRANTS AND DATABASES

SHEILD ME FROM THE SCORN OF SUSPICION

SMITE ALL MY HATERS DEBTORS AND PERPETRATORS

ABSOLVE ME OF FELONIES AND MISDEMEANORS

FORGIVE ME OF THOSE INSTANCES WHEN I HAD GOTTEN CAUGHT

PROVIDE ME WITH THE NECCESSARY STEALTH AND SKILL

BESTOW ME WITH QUICK REFLEXES

YOLK MY SEX TOGETHER WITH YOUR VIOLENCE

I HAVE NO INTEREST IN HEAVEN'S BOUNTIES

NOR THE GUILTS AND SHAMES OF HELL

I AM BUT A SMALL AND MINDLESS CREATURE

WHICH HAS SHED ITS ABSTRACT THOUGHTS AND HUMAN SKIN

AND HAS EXCHANGED ITS SELF-AWARENESS FOR FREEDOM FROM PERCEPTIONS

ALLOW ME TO BE MET WITH BASIC NEEDS

RECIEVE THESE SHAMELESS AND INHUMAN ACTS AS BENEFACTIONS

LET ME BE THE CHANNEL OF YOUR INSTINCT

LET ME BE THE CONDUIT OF YOUR SUPERSPECTRUM

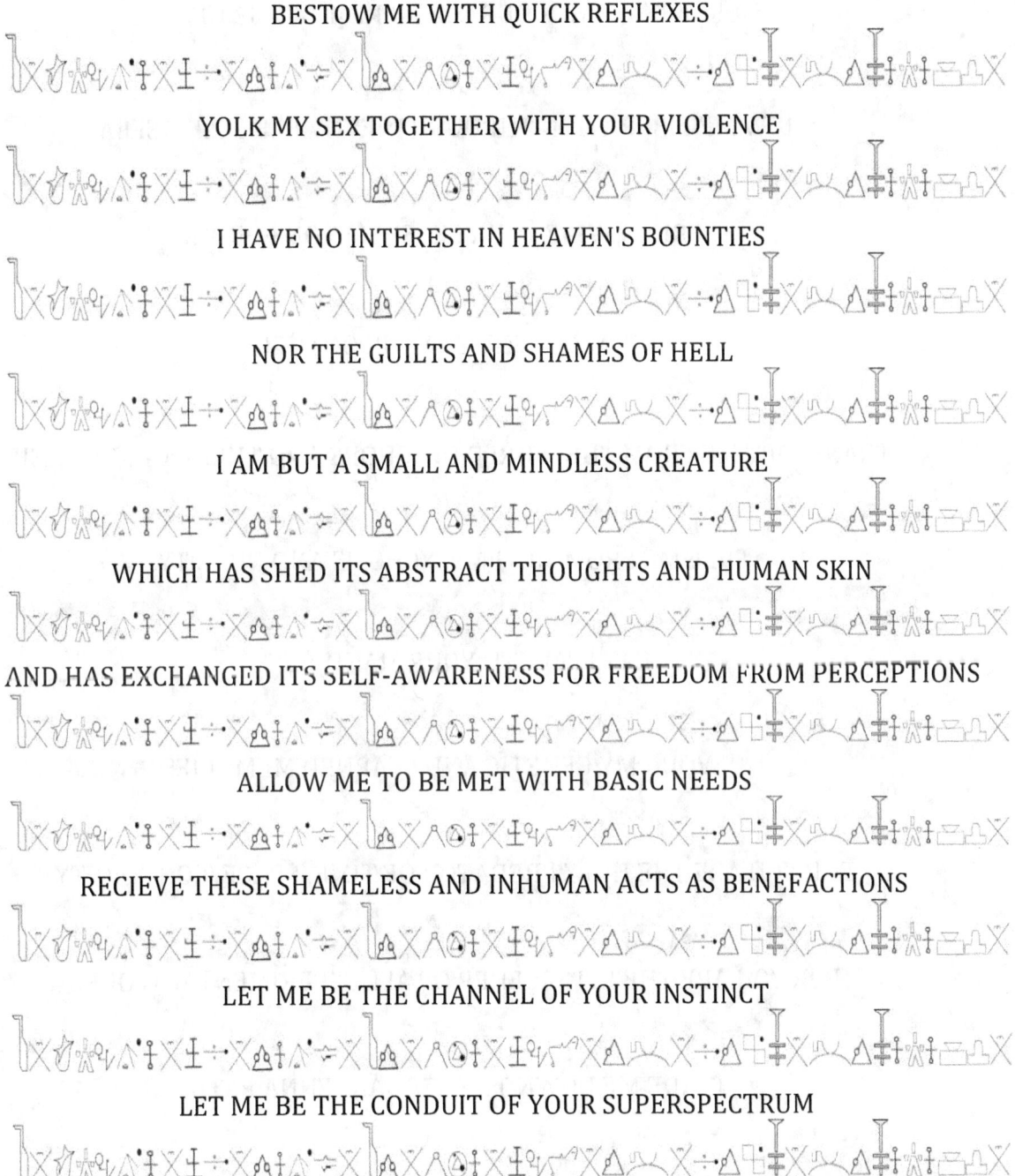

GRANT ME THE COURAGE TO REMOVE MY HEAD

SHOW ME LIBERATION THROUGH INEVITABLE SELF-DEFEAT

SPREAD WIDE YOUR EXOSKELETON FOR ME

LET ME FERTILIZE YOUR OOTHECA

TRANSPORT ME FROM THE WORLD OF ICHORS AND THIS SPOILED FLESH

FREE ME FROM METEMPSYCHOSIS AND DUALITY

EAT ME WITH YOUR MANDIBLES

DEVOUR MY GENETIC AND LEARNED MEMORIES

FOR YOU ARE THE HOLY PREDATOR OF TIME/SPACE/CONTINUITY

FOR YOU ARE THE INTERCEDER OF ALL EXPERIMENTAL WORKS

GUIDE ME DOWN THE LEFT ANTENNA PATH

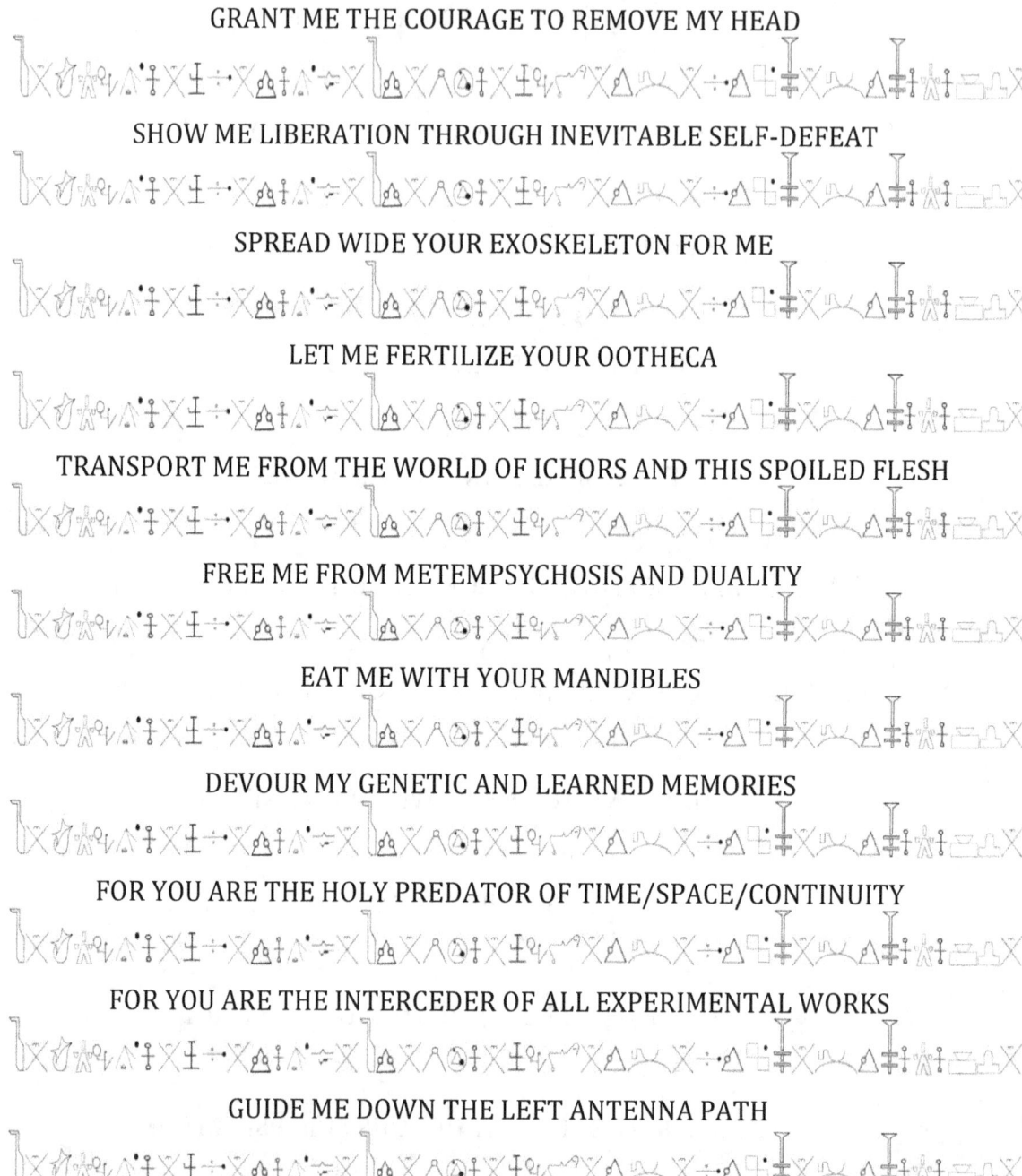

REMOVE YOUR HEAD FOR ME

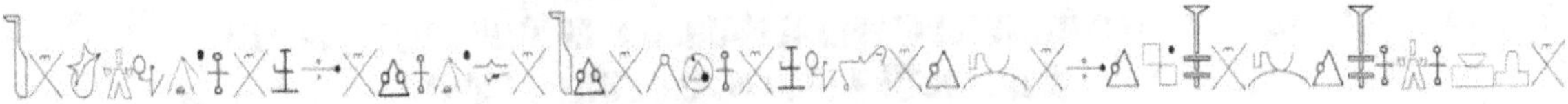

INTERCHANGE IT WITH MY OWN

.

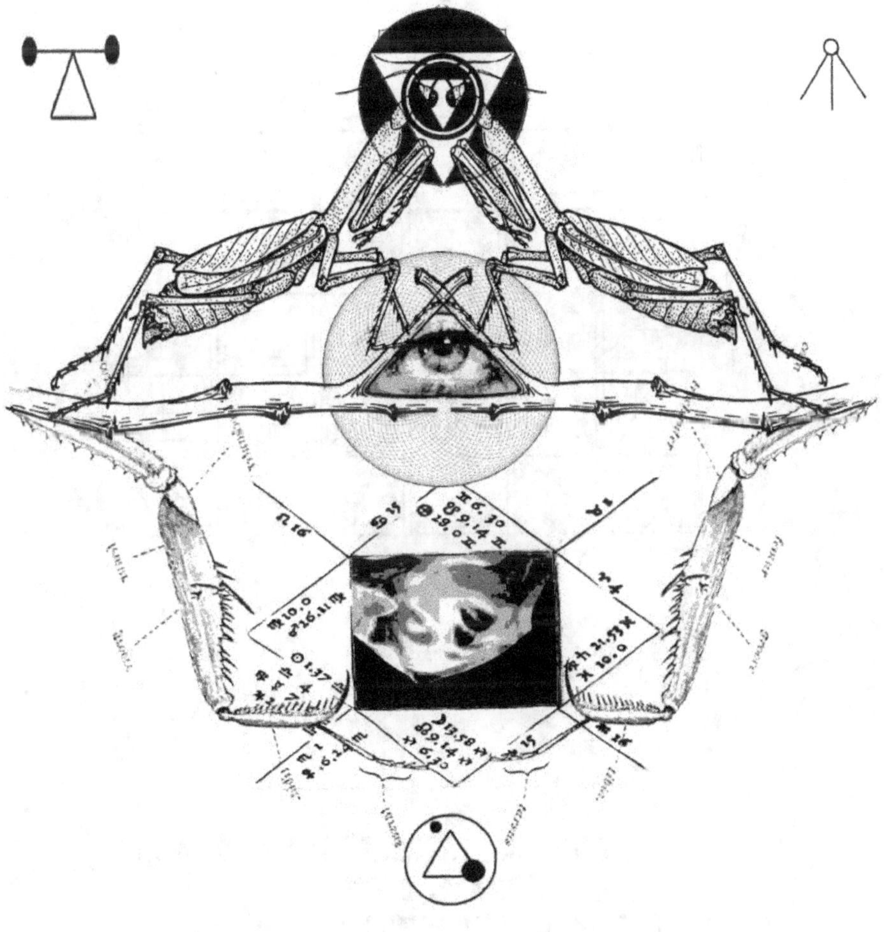

IT IS FABLED
THAT SOLOMON, POWERFUL MAGICIAN-KING OF THE ISREALITES
TRANSFORMED HIS CAMEL INTO A MANTIS
FOR ITS INSOLENCE AND USED THIS SPELL TO BIND IT TO HIS WILL.

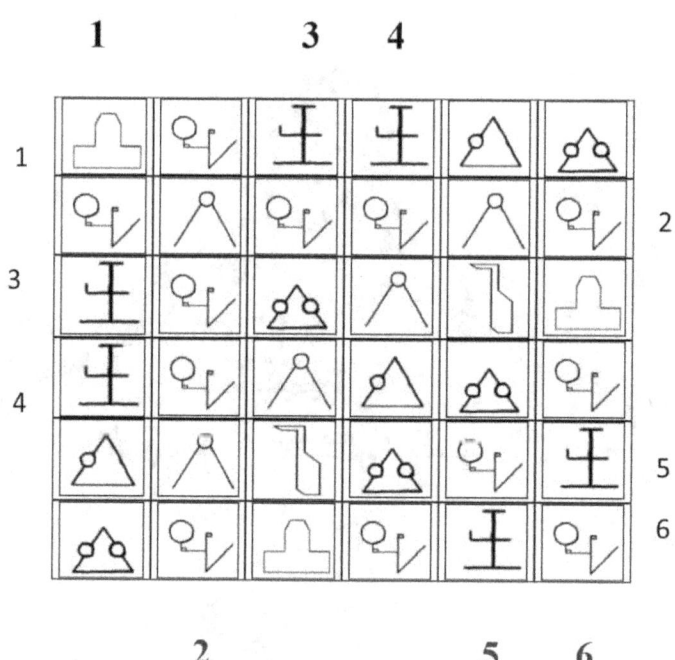

**SOLVE THIS MAGIC SQUARE TO BE USED AS AN
AMULET, BINDING
ONE MANTIS AS A FAMILIAR TO YOURSELF**

1 = PROJECTION MAPS HIGH TO LOW SPATIAL DIMENSIONS

3 = SOLOMON'S CAMEL

4 = A FEMININE HOODLUM

2 = SHADOW, REFLECTION

5 = THIS SPIRIT SPILLS PUTRIFIED LIGHT FROM ITS HAIRS

6 = USTEDES AMASS YOUR EGGS WITH YOUR FROTH

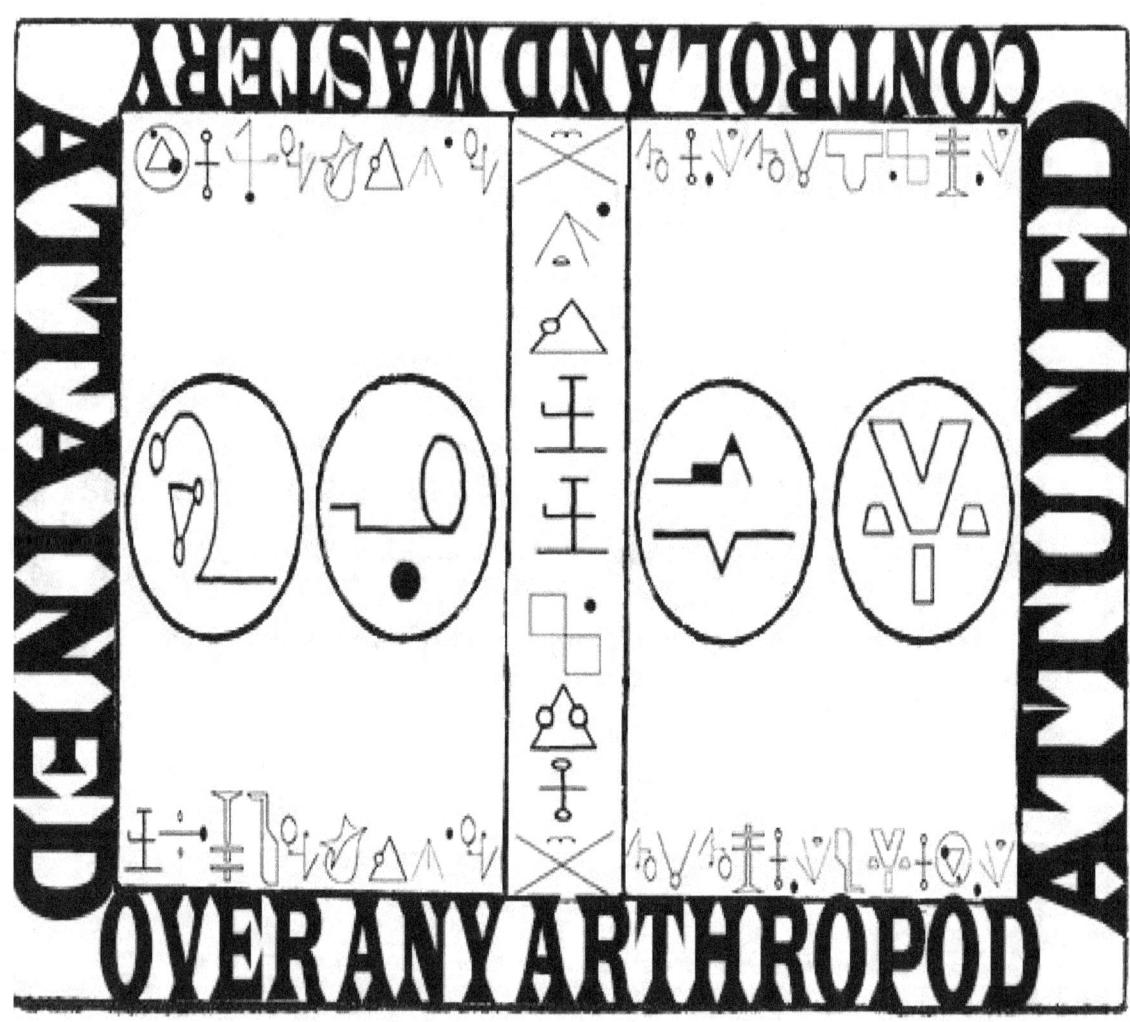

Fig. 1

V
VA
VAL
VALV
VALVA
VALVAI
VALVAIN
VALVAINS
VALVAINSE
VALVAINSEC
VALVAINSECT
VALVAINSECTE
VALVAINSECTEL
VALVAINSECTELO
VALVAINSECTELOR
ALVAINSECTELOR
LVAINSECTELOR
VAINSECTELOR
AINSECTELOR
INSECTELOR
INSECTELO
INSECTEL
INSECTE
INSECT
INSEC
INSE
INS
IN
I

Fig. 2

A

M

R

TOT

I FI

R S R

A N A

G A G

V U R U V

L NTRUN L

A V V A

C A AAA A C

M

Fig. 3

<pre>
                    V
      C   A   AAA   A   C
      A   V   V   A
      L   NTRUN   L
      V   U   R   U V
           G   A   G
           A   N   A
           R   S   R
              I F I
              TOT
               R
               M
               A
</pre>

(*a*) The Symbols of this Segment are manifested by way of an embodiment of Iele, which is not an actual name for this creature, but an epithet or characteristic. Other monikers are as follows:

Dânse, Drăgaice, Vâlve, Iezme, Izme, Irodiţe, Rusalii, Nagode, Vântoase, Domniţe, Măiestre, Frumoase, Muşate, Fetele Codrului, Împărătesele Văzduhului, Zânioare, Sfinte de noapte, Şoimane, Mândre, Fecioare, Albe, Hale, etc. But there are also personal names which appear: *Ana, Bugiana, Dumernica, Foiofia, Lacargia, Magdalina, Ruxanda, Tiranda, Trandafira, Rudeana, Ruja, Păscuţa, Cosânzeana, Orgisceana, Lemnica, Roşia, Todosia, Sandalina, Margalina, Savatina, Rujalina,* etc.

Reciting these epithets result in miracles or curses, depending on the manner in which they are arranged.

(*b*) Vâlva Insectelor executes the Signs and Operations of this Segment.

(*c*) FAMILIAR MANTISES cannot execute the Operations of this Segment.

(d) Let the being, whether man or animal, see the Symbol, and then touch them suddenly with it; they will appear transformed, but this is only a kind of fascination. When you wish to make it cease, place the Symbol upon the head and strike it sharply with a **mounting pin**. Vâlva Insectelor will ensure that things resume their ordinary condition.

(e) Its optional to accompany your actions with this Romanian enchantment:

Mă angajez să întuneric Vâlva Insectelor. Nu voi mai umbla printre oameni. În cazul în care mâinile mele ar trebui să fie, nu va fi gheare. Mi-aş dori să-şi verse forma mea umană în spatele şi a devenit unul dintre voi, un călugăriţă. Aceasta este voinţa mea, aşa praf sa fie!

= I pledge myself to Valve of the Insects. No longer will I walk among humans. Where my hands should be, there will be claws. I wish to shed my human form behind and become one of you, a praying mantis. This is my will, so mote it be!

(**f**) Fig. 1 contains expanding and diminishing Words of Power. VALVAINSECTELOR is evidently from the Romanian Vâlva + Insectelor = Valve of the Insects (literally, "she who controls the ebb and flow of insects"). Fig. 2 and Fig. 3 are atypical Acrostics which function secondarily as Sigils.

† ‡

Fig. 2 rearranges the Romanian incantation,
Vâlva mă va transforma într-un călugăriță
= Vâlva will turn **me** into a praying mantis.

Fig. 3 rearranges another Romanian incantation,
Vâlva va transforma într-un călugăriță
= Vâlva will turn **you** into a praying mantis.

‡ †

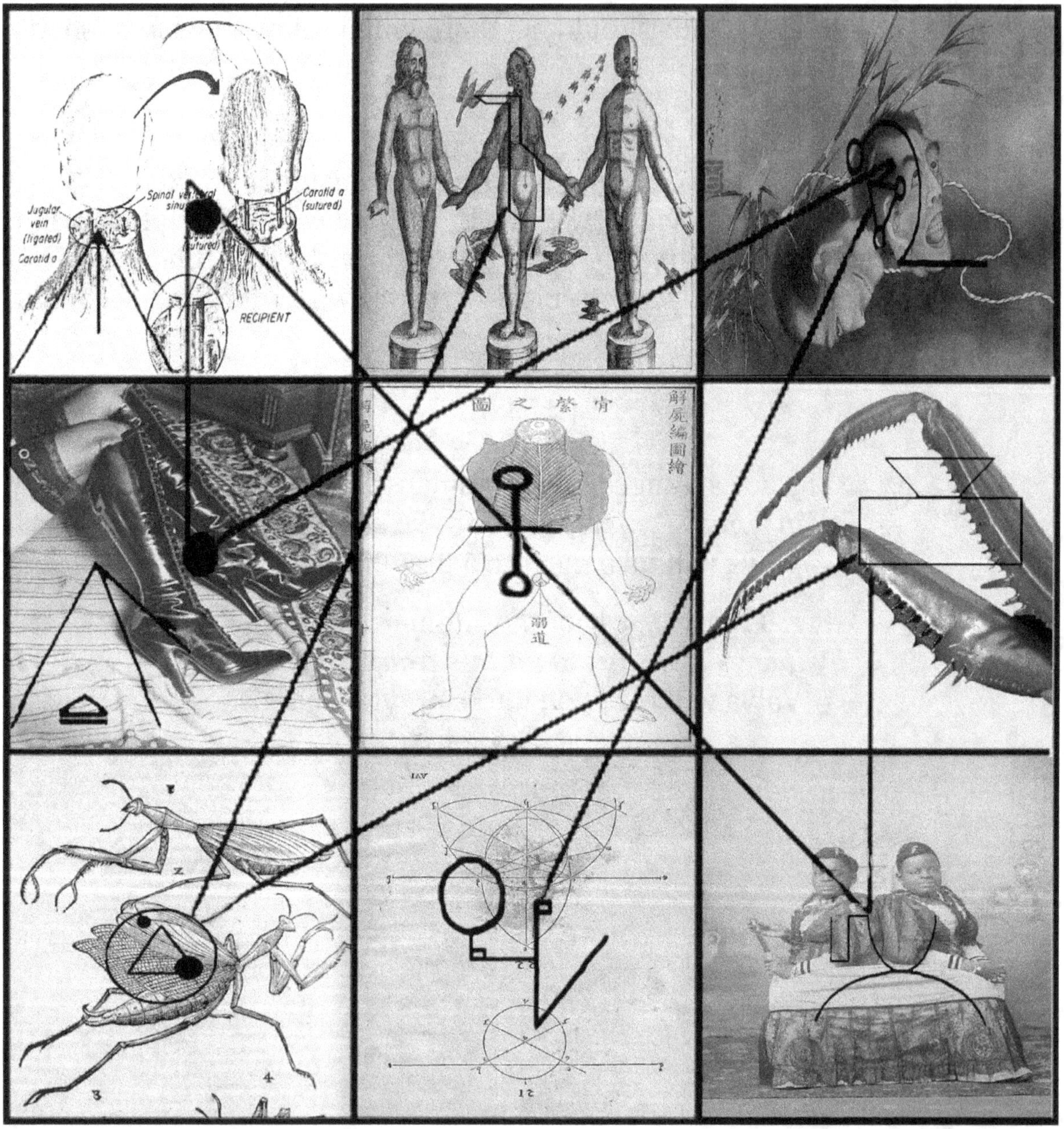
Jugular vein (ligated)
Carotid a
Carotid a (sutured)
RECIPIENT
肯綮之圖

Michaël	Gabriel	Samael	Raphaël	Sachiel	Anaël	Cassiel
Sorath	Lucifer	Bartzabel	Taphthartharath	Hismael	Kedemel	Zazel

HEAR THE DRONING SONGS OF HER MACHINERY WHICH LEVITATE THE PYRAMIDS OF SATURN

AT THE 6TH HOUR OF THE NIGHT, MAY THE INSECT-DEMON ZAZEL VISIT YOU WITHIN THE BODY OF A MANTIS SO THAT HE CAN GRANT FAMILIARS, TELEPORTATIONS, AND TRANSMIT THE SECRET KNOWLEDGE OF HIS LORE

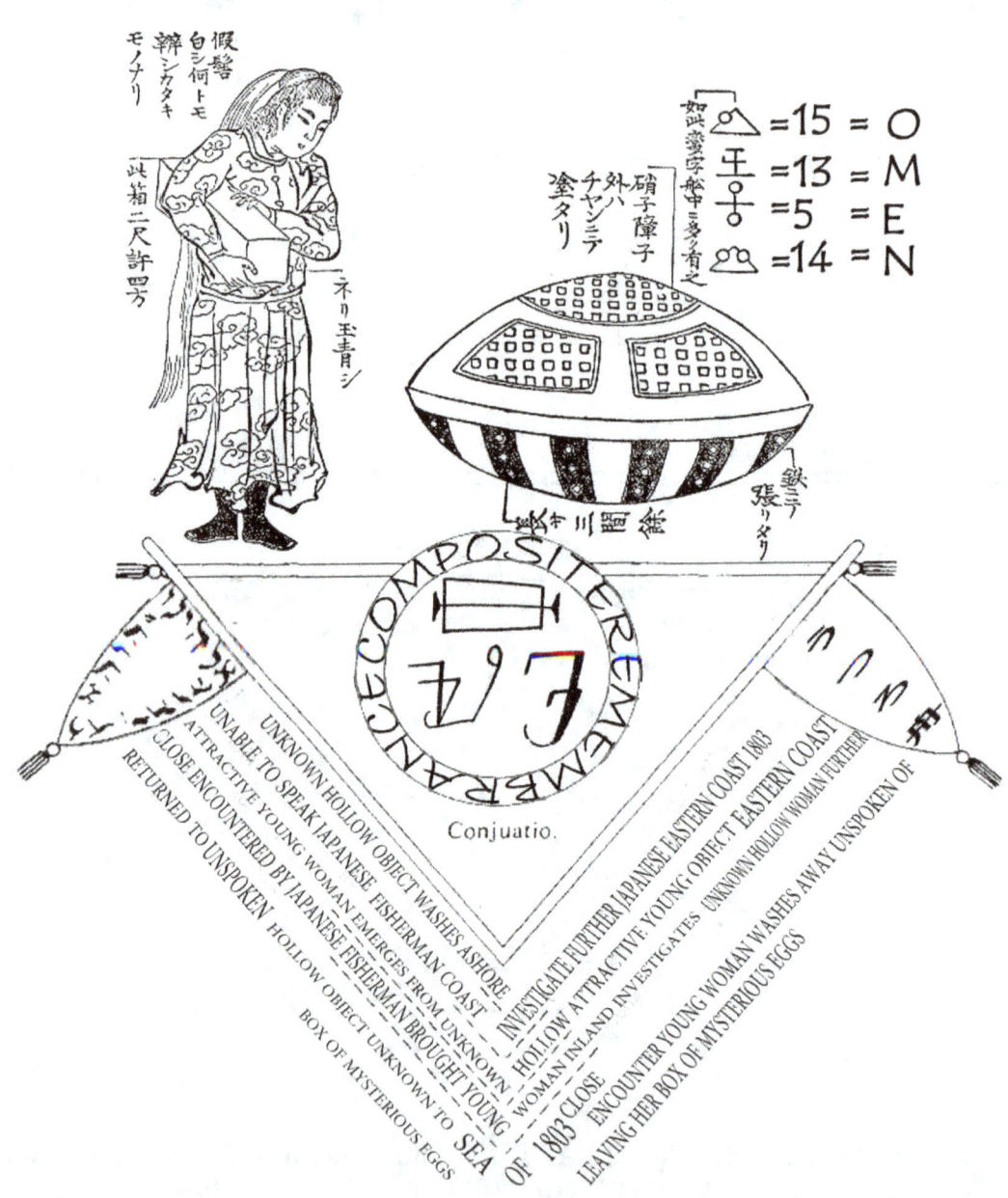

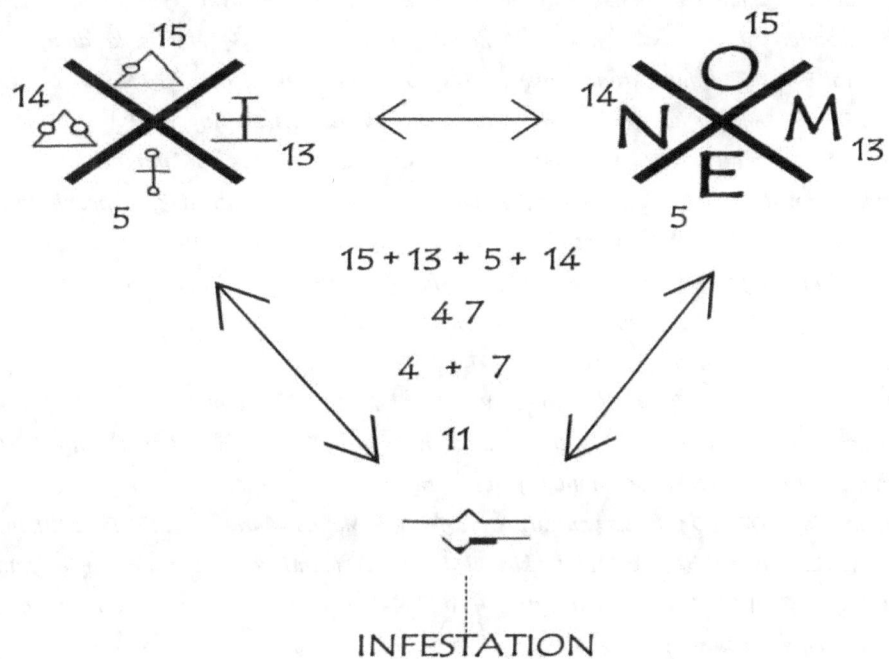

$$15 + 13 + 5 + 14$$

$$4\ 7$$

$$4 + 7$$

$$11$$

INFESTATION

MAY THESE EQUATIONS
SEND THE INSECT-ANGEL CASSIEL—IN THE FORM OF THE UTSURO-BUNE MAIDEN—TO WASH
ASHORE WITHIN THE DREAMS OF YOUR DETRACTORS, AND, WITH SPEED,
MAY SHE INFEST THEM WITH HER EGGS TO HATCH AND PREY UPON THEIR MINDS

108 TAXONOMIC NAMES OF THE INSECT GODESS

ॐ Mantis chhinnamastayai नम: | ॐ Mantis mahavidyayai नम: |
ॐ Mantis mahabhimayai नम: | ॐ Mantis mahodaryai नम: | ॐ Mantis chandeshvaryai नम: | ॐ Mantis chandamatre नम: | ॐ Mantis chandamundaprabhanjinyai नम: | ॐ Mantis mahachandayai नम: | ॐ Mantis chandarupayai नम: | ॐ Mantis chandikayai नम: | ॐ Mantis chandakhandinyai नम: | ॐ Mantis krodhinyai नम: | ॐ Mantis krodhajananyai नम: | ॐ Mantis krodharupayai नम: | ॐ Mantis kuhvai नम: | ॐ Mantis kalayai नम: | ॐ Mantis kopaturayai नम: | ॐ Mantis kopayutayai नम: | ॐ Mantis kopasamharakarinyai नम: | ॐ Mantis vajravairochanyai नम: | ॐ Mantis vajrayai नम: | ॐ Mantis vajrakalpayai नम: | ॐ Mantis dakinyai नम: | ॐ Mantis dakinikarmaniratayai नम: | ॐ Mantis dakinikarmapujitayai नम: | ॐ Mantis dakinisanganiratayai नम: | ॐ Mantis dakinipremapuritayai नम: | ॐ Mantis khatvangadharinyai नम: | ॐ Mantis kharvayai नम: | ॐ Mantis khadgakhapparadharinyai नम: | ॐ Mantis pretashanayai नम: | ॐ Mantis pretayutayai नम: | ॐ Mantis pretasangaviharinyai नम: | ॐ Mantis chhinnamundadharayai नम: | ॐ Mantis chhinnachandavidyayai नम: | ॐ Mantis chitrinyai नम: | ॐ Mantis ghorarupayai नम: | ॐ Mantis ghoradrishtayai नम: | ॐ Mantis ghoraravayai नम: | ॐ Mantis ghanodaryai नम: | ॐ Mantis yoginyai नम: | ॐ Mantis yoganiratayai नम: | ॐ Mantis japayagyaparayanayai नम: | ॐ Mantis yonichakramayyai नम: | ॐ Mantis yonyai नम: | ॐ Mantis yonichakrapravartinyai नम: | ॐ Mantis yonimudrayai नम: | ॐ Mantis yonigamyayai नम: | ॐ Mantis yoniyantranivasinyai नम: | ॐ Mantis yantrarupayai नम: | ॐ Mantis yantramayyai नम: | ॐ Mantis yantreshyai नम: | ॐ Mantis yantrapujitayai नम: | ॐ Mantis kirtyayai नम: | ॐ Mantis kapardinyai नम: | ॐ Mantis kalyai नम: | ॐ Mantis kankalyai नम: | ॐ Mantis kalakarinyai नम: | ॐ Mantis araktayai नम: | ॐ Mantis raktanayanayai नम: | ॐ Mantis raktapanaparayanayai नम: | ॐ Mantis bhavanyai नम: | ॐ Mantis bhutidayai नम: | ॐ Mantis bhutyai नम: | ॐ Mantis bhutidatryai नम: | ॐ Mantis bhairavyai नम: | ॐ Mantis bhairavacharaniratayai नम: | ॐ Mantis bhutabhairavasevitayai नम: | ॐ Mantis bhimayai नम: | ॐ Mantis bhimeshvaryai devyai नम: | ॐ Mantis bhimanadaparayanayai नम: | ॐ Mantis bhavaradhyayai नम: | ॐ Mantis bhavanutayai नम: | ॐ Mantis bhavasagaratarinyai नम: | ॐ Mantis bhadrakalyai नम: | ॐ Mantis bhadratanave नम: | ॐ Mantis bhadrarupayai नम: | ॐ Mantis bhadrikayai नम: | ॐ Mantis bhadrarupayai नम: | ॐ Mantis mahabhadrayai नम: | ॐ Mantis subhadrayai नम: | ॐ Mantis bhadrapalinyai नम: | ॐ Mantis subhavyayai नम: | ॐ Mantis bhavyavadanayai नम: | ॐ Mantis sumukhyai नम: | ॐ Mantis siddhasevitayai नम: | ॐ Mantis siddhidayai नम: | ॐ Mantis siddhinivahayai नम: | ॐ Mantis siddhayai नम: | ॐ Mantis siddhanishevitayai नम: | ॐ Mantis shubhadayai नम: | ॐ Mantis shubhagayai नम: | ॐ Mantis shuddhayai नम: | ॐ Mantis shuddhasattvayai नम: | ॐ Mantis shubhavahayai नम: | ॐ Mantis shreshthayai नम: | ॐ Mantis drishtimayyai नम: | ॐ Mantis devyai नम: | ॐ Mantis drishtisamharakarinyai नम: | ॐ Mantis sharvanyai नम: | ॐ Mantis sarvagayai नम: | ॐ Mantis sarvayai नम: | ॐ Mantis sarvamangalakarinyai नम: | ॐ Mantis shivayai नम: | ॐ Mantis shantayai नम: |
ॐ Mantis shantirupayai नम: | ॐ Mantis mridanyai नम: | ॐ Mantis madanaturayai नम: |

TOUCH AND GAZE UPON THIS

AS AN INCARNATION

OF YOURSELF

TOUCH AND GAZE UPON THIS

Mantis yantrapujitayai
Mantis kirtyayai
Mantis kapardinyai
Mantis kalyai
Mantis kankalyai
Mantis kalakarinyai
Mantis araktayai
Mantis raktanayanayai
Mantis raktapanaparayanayai
Mantis bhavanyai
Mantis bhutidayai
Mantis bhutyai
Mantis bhutidatryai
Mantis bhairavyai
Mantis bhairavacharaniratayai
Mantis bhutabhairavasevitayai
Mantis bhimayai
Mantis bhimeshvaryai-devyai
Mantis bhimanadaparayanayai
Mantis bhavaradhyayai
Mantis ghorarupayai
Mantis ghoradrishtayai
Mantis ghoraravayai
Mantis ghanodaryai
Mantis yoginyai
Mantis yoganiratayai
Mantis yonichakramayyai
Mantis yonyai
Mantis yonichakrapravartinyai
Mantis yonimudrayai
Mantis yonigamyayai
Mantis yonigyantranivasinyai
Mantis yantravrupayai
Mantis yantramayyai
Mantis yantreshyai

SEAL EMBRACING GRIEF AND

TRAUMAS OF REDEATH AS OUR

DEFINING SIGNATURES IN TIME

TOUCH AND GAZE UPON THIS

INSECT CAN EMBODY HER

COSMIC MECHANICAL MIND

SEAL SO THAT YOUR FAMILIAR

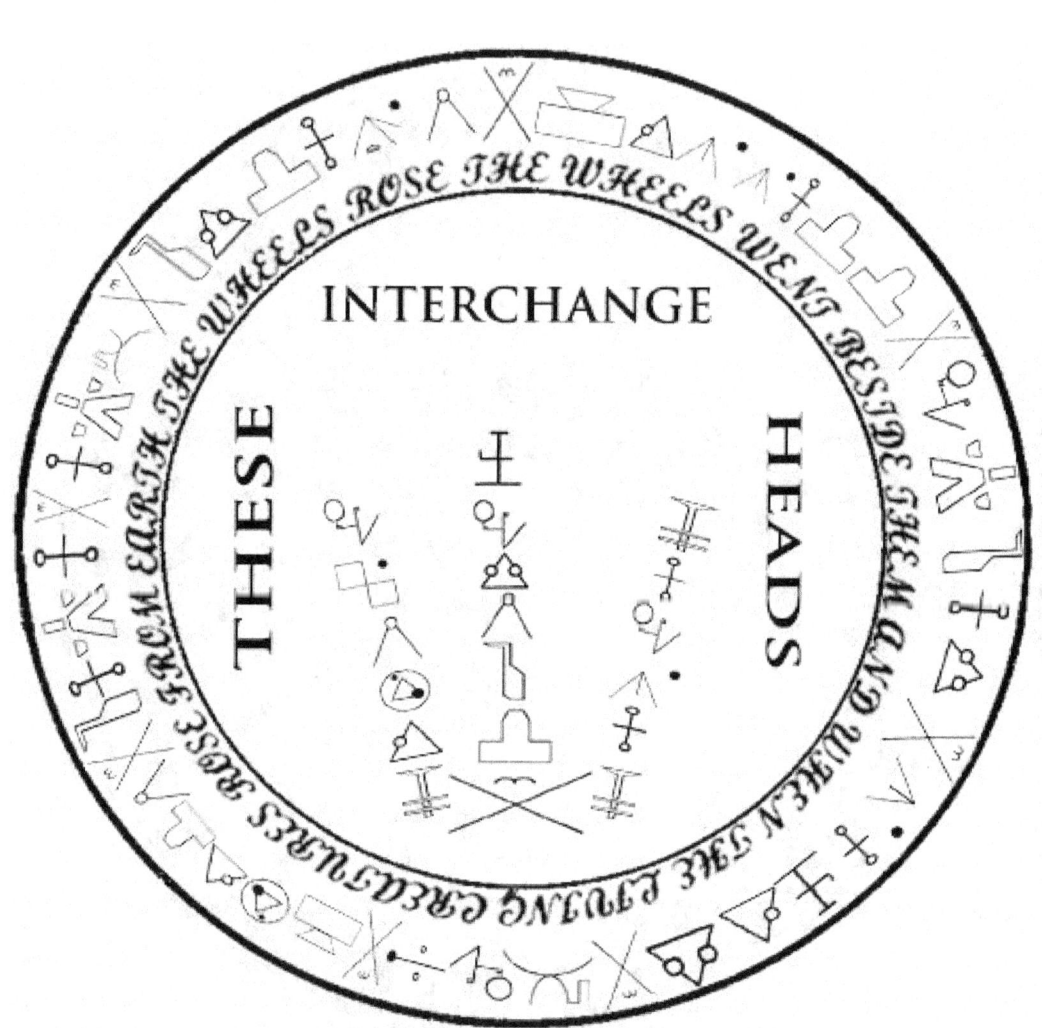

INTERCHANGE

THESE

HEADS

FROM EARTH THE WHEELS ROSE THE WHEELS WENT BESIDE THEM AND WHEN THE FLYING CREATURES ROSE

IN ALL REFERENCES TO HEAD REMOVAL AND/OR EXCHANGE WITHIN THIS SEGMENT IT IS QUITE LITERALLY OF VITAL IMPORTANCE TO UNDERSTAND THAT ALL HEADS IN QUESTION ARE NOT PHYSICAL HEADS BUT SUBTLE HEADS THAT SHOULD ONLY EFFECT PARTICIPANTS' AWARENESSES OF HEADNESS OR HEADLESSNESS ONCE THE SUBTLE HEAD HAS BEEN REMOVED AND/OR EXCHANGED.

Like those twig magic workings used in Palo Mayombe,
the exuvia, or molted exoskeleton of arthropods,
are crushed or ground into a powder...

Northern Expedition of Exuvia Per Air

After the powder of this specialized cuticle is magically activated by one initiated in the arts of arthropodomancy, it is to be set out into the air while facing North. A compass may be utilized for this particular work. While standing in a clearing or from a great height, with the arthropodomancer positioned firmly in one place, the powdered exuvia may be blown into the air with the intention of making contact with a desired person, place, or thing. Perform this mode with clear intentions to work in the favor or misfortune of a the designated target.

Eastern Expedition of Exuvia Per Fire

While facing the direction of the rising sun, the exuvia is first prepared by soaking in a flammable liquid or in an alcoholic drink. Everclear, which yields the highest percentage of ethanol for human consumption, is considered the optimal medium for this by the arthropodomancer majority. However, lighter fluid has a similarly good effect. The exuvia is then set ablaze. The soaked, molted exoskeleton can be burned in the practitioner's skull cup made from the head of a man who died a violent death, either whole or in the form of crushed matter. Exuviae are typically burned outdoors (preferably within a vibrant bone yard) to symbolize its newly-granted liberty to travel through the world to carry out a magical work by whatever means that it desires.

Southern Expedition of Exuvia Per Water

Boil the exuvia in its entirety or crushed. The arthropodally charged water may be poured into a bottle to be tossed or sprayed Southerly. As an alternative method, activated water can be added into foods or beverages to be ingested by a person for either of these intended outcomes: benefit or harm. This is a necessary yet (perhaps intentionally?) undocumented ingredient used by Hoodoos for the infamous *Live Things In You* spell— the cause for manifesting living, squirming arthropods (or other vermin) within whomever it's administered.

Western Expedition of Exuvia Per Earth

Exuvia may be used as a "crossing powder"—a powder that's intended to be tread on or stepped over—once dispensed upon the ground or buried in the dirt whilst facing the setting sun. Amassing the exuvia with mud or any other solid moldable material (including feces) is also influential when thrown directly at a living or nonliving target. In this mode, it is also smeared upon a doorway to bring certain luck or ruin to the business or the household.

***

***

An exuvia adopts the qualities of the arthropod who's liberated it as a commemorative monument of its generally short existence. Logically, there is a transference of quality and virtue that passes from any arthropod into its cuticle. for example, exuviae of mantises are rich in stealth, precision, cunning, and speed. Yet, the identification of any exuvia's individualistic qualities should be left to the discernment of the arthropodomancer—who must first go mad in order to discern. The arthropodomancer must go mad because the madness of arthropodomancy is that it adds the madness of the idea of magical dispensation of the exuvia to the madness of the practitioner who's working it so that the magical reality of any spell increases. The practitioner will fail at casting these, or any other kind of spells, unless they are maddened and pray madly over the exuvia because it is, in essence, madcap to assign intent to prayer words, whether spoken or recorded, or to assume these words could dictate any physical component of a charm to carry out its task.

:::LIBER EXUVIA:::
BEHOLD, THIS MADCAP PRAYER:

‡† †‡

M M M M M M

U U U U U U

T T T T T

A A A A A A

T T T T T T

I I I I I I

S S S S S S

I I I I I I

D D D D D D

N N N N N N

A A A A A A

T T T T T

U U U U U U

M M M M M M

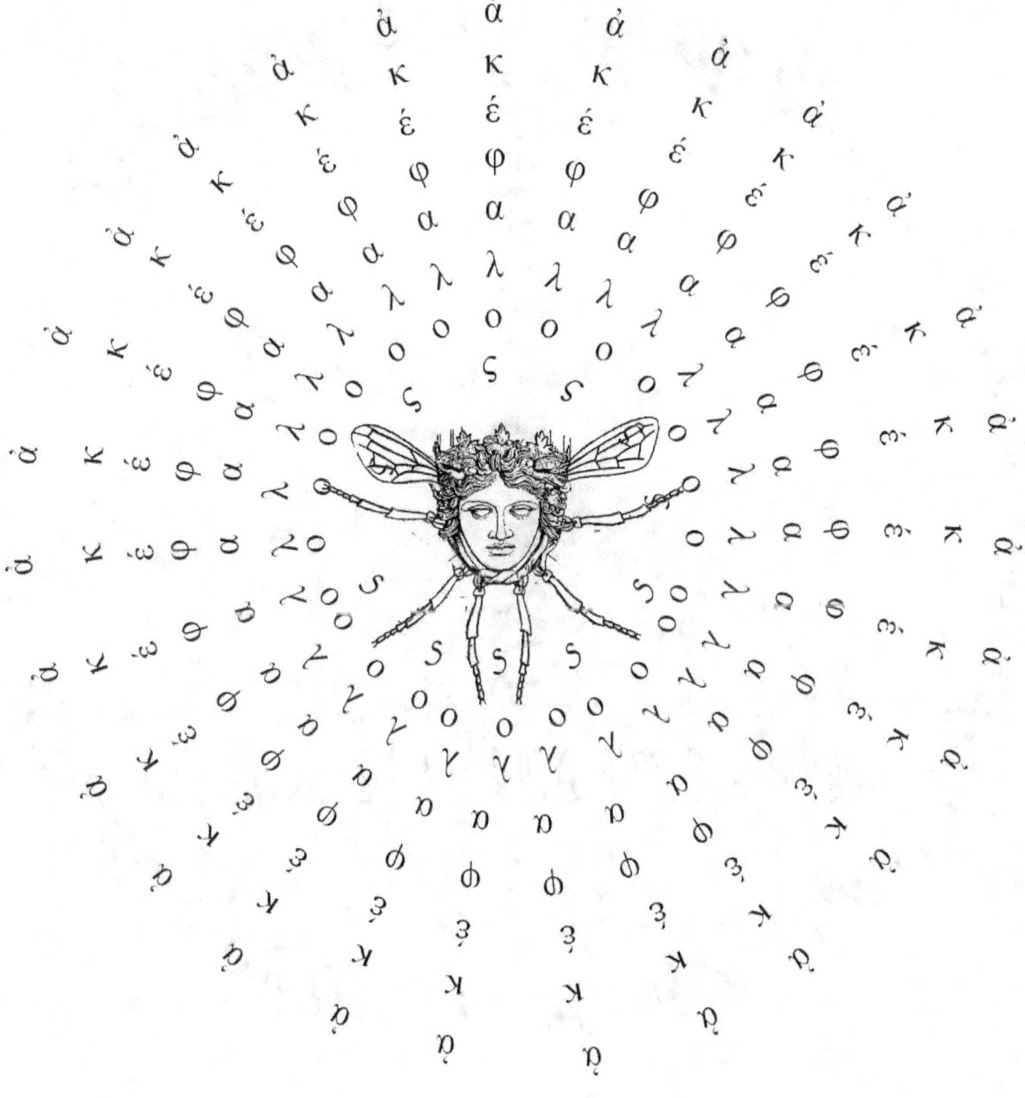
ἀκέφαλος

PLAYING A ROLEPLAYING GAME THE MAGICIAN DECODING A GAMEMORE AND THE GAMER'S PLAYING A

ENDLESS SCHOLAR

SHOW ME THE DIFFERENCE BETWEEN

SHOWMETHEDIFFERENCEBETWEEN

SHOWMETHEDIFFERENCEBETWEEN

SHOWMETHEDIFFERENCEBETWEEN

SHOWMETHEDIFFERENCEBETWEEN

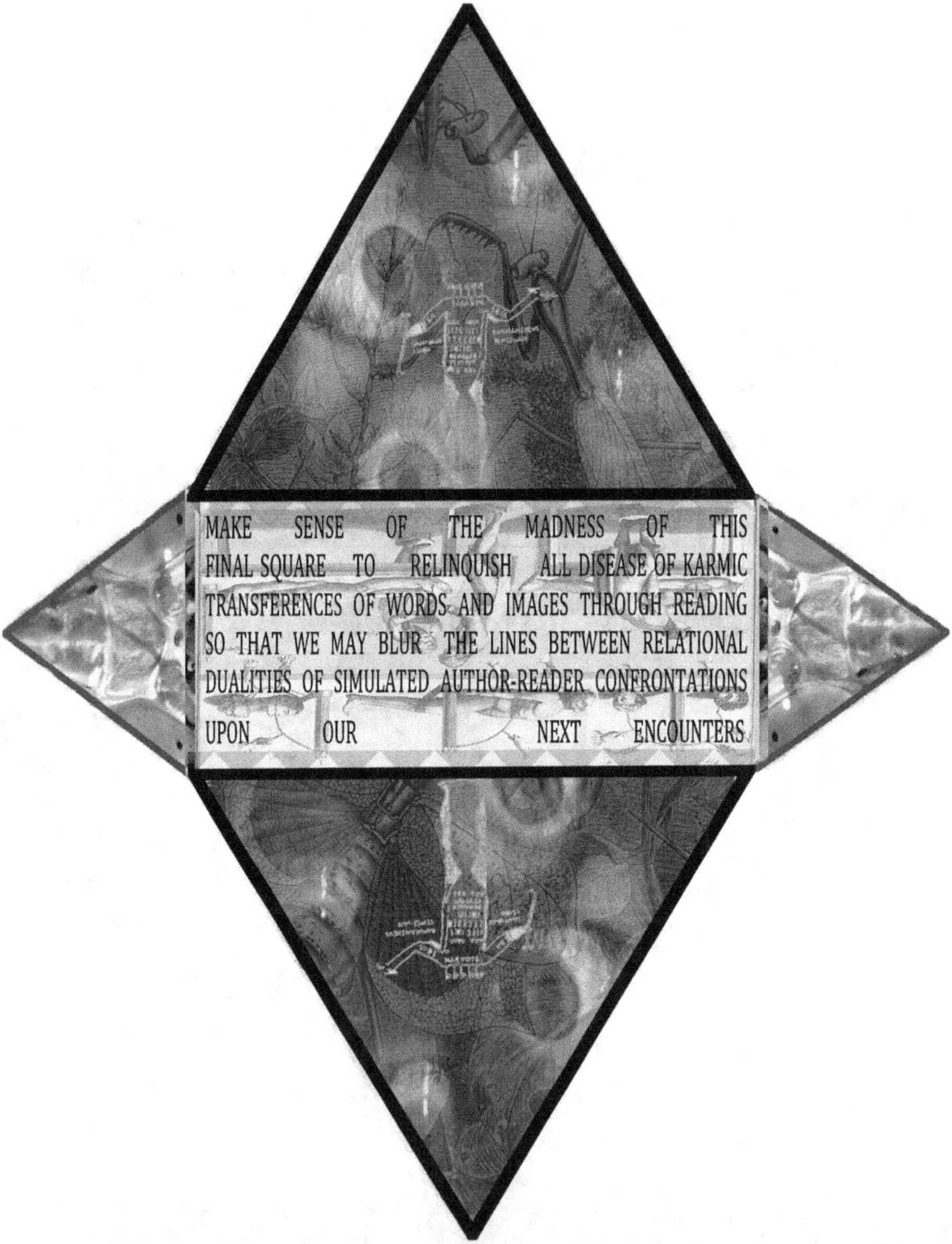

MAKE SENSE OF THE MADNESS OF THIS
FINAL SQUARE TO RELINQUISH ALL DISEASE OF KARMIC
TRANSFERENCES OF WORDS AND IMAGES THROUGH READING
SO THAT WE MAY BLUR THE LINES BETWEEN RELATIONAL
DUALITIES OF SIMULATED AUTHOR-READER CONFRONTATIONS
UPON OUR NEXT ENCOUNTERS

other titles from gnOme

A & N ● *Autophagiography*

Annabella of Ely ● *Annabella of Ely: Poems I-LXVII*

Brian O'Blivion ● *Blackest Ever Hole*

Cergat ● *Earthmare: The Lost Book of Wars*

Erba ● *The Walk of Absence*

Eva Clanculator ● *Atheologica Germanica*

Ars Cogitanda ● *footnote to silence*

Maure Coise ● *Geophilosophical Branding*

The Filatory: Compendium I

The Lost Couplets of Pir Iqbal the Impaled

M ● *Un-Sight/ Un-Sound (delirium X.)*

M.O.N. ● *ObliviOnanisM*

oudeís● *the spiral consilience*

The Proverbs of Ashendōn

Pseudo-Leopardi ● *Cantos for the Crestfallen*

I. P. Snooks ● *Be Still, My Throbbing Tattoo*

Rasu-Yong Tugen, Baroness de Tristeombre ● *A Natural History of Seaweed Dreams*

Rasu-Yong Tugen, Baroness De Tristeombre ● *Songs from the Black Moon*

Subject A ● *Verses from the Underlands*

Y.O.U. ● *How to Stay in Hell*

HWORDE

Ambroise Lefurgey: Selected Poems

Nab Saheb and Denys X. Arbaris ● *Bergmetal: Oro-Emblems of the Musical Beyond*

N ● *Hemisphere Eleven*

gnOme is a secret press specializing in the publication of anonymous, pseudepigraphical, and apocryphal works from past, present, and future.

"The less the head, the more the wound will heal. No head there is no wound. Live a headless life. Move as a total being, and accept things" (Osho).

gnOme is acephalic. Book sales support the authors.

GNOMEBOOKS.WORDPRESS.COM

www.ingramcontent.com/pod-product-compliance
Lightning Source LLC
Chambersburg PA
CBHW082047220626
47052CB00007B/1245